PRAISE FOR MJ JAMES

James's effective worldbuilding employs strong emotional and sensory descriptions ... often paralleling our society's own issues with neuro-divergence, gender equality, economic disparity, and more.

THE BOOKLIFE PRIZE ON THE IMMORTAL PART OF MYSELF

Good world-building and a storyline I was quickly hooked into.

GOODREADS REVIEWER ON IN-BETWEEN

This book was so deep.I cried throughout it. If you're looking for something with similar vibes to A Handmaiden's Tale but sci-fi, this is your book.

GOODREADS REVIEWER ON THE IMMORTAL PART OF MYSELF

LENNON

EMBER TOWN SERIES
BOOK 5

MJ JAMES

Edited by Sam Willow
Proofread by Erica Bell
Cover design by MJ James (No AI Usage)

E-book ISBN: 978-1-958175-25-5
Paperback ISBN: 978-1-958175-32-3

CONTENT WARNING

Lennon talks about loss of community due to identity and contains C-PTSD moments.

Lennon Contains
  Abandonment of community
  Ableism
  Homophobia

ALSO BY MJ JAMES

In-Between

The Immortal Part of Myself

NeurodiVeRse

Inside a Dark Space

The Ember Town Series

Lucas

Phoenix

Birk

Mika

Lennon

Rays of light bent through the tree line as the sun lowered in the sky, resulting in patches of brightness followed by shadow as he moved on the narrow mountain road. The road was barely large enough to fit two cars, and Len was grateful he was on the side next to the mountain. The other side followed a cliff so deep that he could not see the end of it. There was just a small gravel shoulder between the road and a never-ending spiral through the trees. He would survive the crash—probably—he was a werewolf, after all, but it wouldn't be pleasant. Len pressed on, the light dancing in his vision.

He glanced in his rearview mirror. The car was still there. It was a white sedan that had been behind him since he had hit the mountain pass. That wasn't abnormal. There was no other way to go out here to these tiny towns in the Rocky Mountains. Len hadn't come across another road for miles.

It was just that he had seen a similar car pull out of

the rental car company back at the Denver airport. He had, of course, passed a few similar-looking vehicles as he'd driven down the freeway. Then one had turned off with him to this rural road leading back to Ember, his current assignment.

Len couldn't be sure it was the same car. He wasn't all that great with cars, and he hadn't glimpsed the driver. Still …

His phone was stuck in his pocket. Len hadn't connected it to the rental car. Often, he never did. It was too much hassle when he would be returning the car the next morning. Now he wished he could easily call someone, if only to have them on the phone as he drove down this desolate road.

The car seemed to creep up on him, the bumper edging closer to his own, and Len slowed. He tried to catch sight of the driver through his rearview mirror, but all he saw was white skin and black hair before the other car backed off.

Who was he kidding? He didn't have anyone to call. One more paranoid phone call to Danni, his contact at the organization, and he risked losing his job. He couldn't lose his job. It was all he had.

He reached over, turned on the radio, and jerked as the speakers let out a loud burst of static. He set it to scan through the stations, the numbers rolling through as he kept driving, never settling down. Eventually, he shut it off again.

The car was still behind him. Of course it was— there hadn't been a break in the mountain road.

The built-in navigation system showed there was

still over an hour before he reached his final destination. That was plenty of time for the car to turn off on a side road, and the thought settled his mind. Len tried to focus on driving and not get distracted by the glint of the sun's rays as they fragmented from the tree limbs.

It reminded him of the meme—the one with the dog that kept shouting "squirrel" every time it re-saw the same squirrel. His mind worked the same way, at times, choosing to pay attention to whatever was the shiniest.

It also led him to obsess over details others didn't think were important. Danni had told him it made him paranoid, and it was getting in the way of him doing his job. Maybe she was right, but that didn't help the feeling in his gut that something was wrong.

As the road started to open up, allowing a passing lane, Len got over to the right. He kept his eyes glued to his mirror, waiting for the white car to finally pass him. Instead, it entered the lane behind him.

Len slowed down, his speed dropping from the posted 55 to 45 … then 35. The car stayed behind him. Finally, he went down to 25, hoping that the other vehicle would go past him, allowing his mind to finally be able to focus on the meeting that he had scheduled for that night.

Instead, other cars started to appear, a spaced-out line that must have been hidden by the mountain curves. A few honked at him. One even rolled down the passenger window so he could see their middle finger. The white car stayed close behind.

His heart started racing. Blood pounded through his

body, and before he knew what he was doing, he pushed on the accelerator, trying to build up enough speed to catch up to the cars that had passed him before the lanes closed up again.

His speed increased from 55 to 65 and finally up to 85, allowing him to pass a few cars just as the lanes merged back together. The car behind him drove up to his bumper, laying on its horn. All Len cared about was that he could no longer see the white car.

He started to relax and enjoy the drive, staying in the middle of the pack as a few dropped off once they started to pass highways heading up to other mountain towns. As Len turned onto the road leading to Ember, only one other car turned off—a white sedan.

His breath caught, and his hands started to sweat. It was fifteen minutes to Ember. Len thought about pulling off the road and seeing if the car would pass. Except, what if the other vehicle stopped and whoever was driving it got out while they were in the middle of nowhere? The other cars had all left, so it was just the two of them. Gritting his teeth, Len kept following the directions to his meeting, hoping that somehow this was still all in his head. He was once again being paranoid.

Ember was a small city, which wasn't that surprising. Most magical communities tended to live in small towns or in more isolated areas completely by themselves, in forest glens or closed-off compounds. Anywhere they could carve out an area where they were allowed to be themselves without humans finding out. The organization Len worked for, Eternal Beauty Environmental Protection, was interested in the environment around these magical communities. Although everyone just called it "the organization," as it was one of the few that interacted with all the various magical species. It seemed to be everywhere, but even Len, who had worked for the organization for a decade, wasn't quite sure what they did.

The trees started to gradually drop off as he drove through what he assumed was one of the main roads. He stopped at a four-way stop sign, the white car directly behind him, and followed the directions toward a street full of businesses. Cars were lining the roads, filling up the spots. Families walked along the sidewalks in costumes, children licking suckers or holding pillowcases. Len realized that it was Halloween. It was so hard to keep track of the days when you were constantly in motion.

Ember seemed to go all out for Halloween. Businesses flashed purple, black, and orange lights with carved pumpkins on their stoops. Young adults were decked out in gothic vampire attire. Adults wore their finest clothing, as if it were a celebration, instead of a costume party. Even the children seemed to be dressed in homemade costumes rather than commercial. There was only one superhero in a pack of fairies, witches, and zombies. If Len didn't know better, he would think there was a coven here. But there couldn't be, because only one magical community lived in a territory, and he was here to meet with a nymph.

Len felt the magic congregating around him and

realized that Ember must be a nexus town—a place where ley lines intersected. The energy seeped into him, and his body started to relax. It had been a while since his travels had taken him to a true nexus. Never had he been to a town with so much magical activity.

Rocko's, their meeting place, was to his left, but street parking was full. He turned at the last second, finding a parking lot a few buildings down. It was small, but there was one open spot. Len pulled into it and watched as the white car circled the same parking lot and then left.

He thought about turning around and driving directly back to the airport. Something wasn't right. He could feel it in every part of his body. But Danni would just tell him it was his paranoia, and that he needed to face it full on. He didn't want to face it. What he wanted was someplace where he could feel safe. A place to call his own where he could go to sleep in the same bed, and keep some clothes in the closet instead of having everything he owned in his suitcase and briefcase.

It felt ungrateful even thinking that. The organization had given him a place when he'd had nothing. So, he tried to ignore his tumbling gut and, grabbing his briefcase, got out of the car.

Night was just beginning to fall as he walked back toward the building. Everything seemed quiet, aside from the noise pouring from his destination. It was overflowing with people, most of them in costumes. The night was so full of alcohol fumes that Len was worried about getting drunk by proximity. He hadn't realized they were meeting in a bar. Though it wasn't the first time. Small towns seemed to love their local bars.

Len pulled out his phone and did a quick review of his contact—he really should have done more prep—and headed through the open door.

The bar was full. People stood elbow to elbow, most dressed in costumes, and holding glasses that smelled of alcohol and pumpkin spice mixed in with too much body odor. It was so crowded that there wasn't even a path to walk down. Len had to squeeze between the throngs of people. Whenever he got enough space, he would raise his phone to study the photo again and scan through the faces he could see.

Finally, he spotted them. According to his files, Birk was a nymph. They tended to be a very closely guarded species, but Len had spoken to a few families before. All of them had been perfectly reasonable, but they had all also met him in forest glens and not in a crowded bar.

Birk was sitting at a table, only they weren't alone. Someone else was there with thick brown curly hair and long flowing skirts. If Len hadn't known better, he would have sworn that she was a witch, but having two major species in one town was unheard of. Most likely, she was a human, and Len was best to wait until she left. He stood quietly as they finished their conversation, holding his briefcase in front of him to help stop it from being jostled as people pressed around him.

"Is there something I can help you with?"

Len startled, realizing that the human—no, witch, according to the faint smell of magick that still clung to her—was right next to him.

"I'm Len … I mean Lennon. I have a meeting scheduled with Birk." He tried to pull on his professional persona, using his full name while attempting to exude confidence. It was harder with all the people around him. There were too many smells and noises to be able to know what was happening. People casually brushed past him as he stood, causing him to shudder in reflex. It didn't help that he was already on edge from the drive.

"Len," Birk said. "It is nice to finally meet you in person." They held out their hand, and Len glanced at it, trying to figure out how to get out of shaking it. Thankfully, they seemed not to even notice. "This is … well … This is Mika, the local witches' coven leader. She is also my girlfriend."

It seemed new, like neither had quite gotten used to the idea. Nymphs tended to be fairly open in their sexuality, but all the witches he had met had been more reserved. Except the California coven. He had been sent out to observe them for a week. Even though the coven members had been nice enough, they were a loud group in an even louder city—and the smells. He had been glad when that assignment had ended.

"Mika, this is Len," Birk continued. "He is a representative from the organization that is funding the conservation work I am doing."

The witch held out her hand. He was trying to determine if she would get offended if he gave her a fist bump instead when he caught a smell—werewolves. His body froze, his breath caught, and his mind went blank.

"There are wolves here?" His mouth started working on its own. "There is a coven and a wolf pack here?" He needed to get away before the wolves smelled him, but he had a job to do. He tried to calm his pulse and even out his breathing. He couldn't let them see his terror.

"Right," Len said. "I didn't realize this meeting would be so public. Maybe there is somewhere a little safer we could go?" Anywhere that didn't include other wolves.

He saw them now. There was a group in the back of the room. Most of them seemed unaware that another wolf had joined their ranks. They were too busy trying to get a buzz from the alcohol, and playing darts. Except for one wolf who was staring straight at him. He wasn't an alpha. Len wouldn't have been able to stop himself from running if he had been.

He had dark brown hair that lay slightly messy on his head. His eyes were light brown, reflecting the light from the lamp on the wall. His face was neutral, if intense, but you could tell that it spent more time laughing than frowning. Len felt his temperature rise, his heart pound, and he began to smell his own pheromones. *No, not now, and not with a wolf.* He turned back toward the nymph, trying to distract himself from the other man.

"Don't worry," Birk said. "Rocko's is neutral territory. Even the vampires know better than to cause a scene here. This is the safest place you could be in Ember. If anyone gets out of hand, Rocko will handle it."

Vampires? How are there this many creatures in Ember? Len had grown used to being thrown into unexpected scenarios, but nothing like this. Magical creatures were territorial and lived with their own kind. He had come to see a nymph, and that was all he should have found —not vampires, witches, and certainly not other werewolves. The organization hadn't sent him to see other werewolves.

"Then maybe I should just never leave," he said. Not that he trusted that whoever this Rocko was could protect him from other werewolves. No, what he wanted was to get in his car and drive far away. But that meant going outside and facing whoever had followed him to this town. A new streak of fear rushed through him, and the wolf in the back let out a growl so low that Len was sure no one else could hear it. Len couldn't help the low whimper that he let out as a result. *Why hadn't the organization told him there would be wolves?*

Then the unknown wolf stood and rushed through the herd of people and out the front door. Len was still facing Birk and Mika, so he hadn't seen it play out, but he had heard all of it. The other wolves seemed oblivious to his exit, or Len's existence, and he felt himself relax slightly. However, another part of himself was disappointed as the wolf's scent began to dissipate in the air, lost to alcohol and sweat.

It wasn't until Birk pointed to the empty chair that he realized the witch had left. He sat down, trying to compose himself. He placed his briefcase on the table and pulled out his tablet, turning it on and going to his notes about the current assignment.

He had meant to review the notes on the plane, but his previous assignment had been a banshee. The corporation was interested in the impact on the new region as a result of her immigration with her attached family. Except, last night, she had gotten lost in a lament for the soon-to-be death of a family member. Len had stayed up with her, listening to her tears. Instead of studying on the plane, he had fallen asleep.

The banshee had texted while he was in the air. There had been a car accident, and one of the young men in the family had been lost.

"Would you like something to drink? Maybe some food? Rocko is an amazing cook."

Len looked up from his notes, almost having forgotten he was not alone. "No, thank you. The organization had some questions about some of your recent reports. It won't take up too much of your time, so you can continue with your evening."

"You've had dinner, then?"

"Well, I didn't have a chance. The flight arrived late, and I hadn't realized it would be such a long drive. I will pick up something after we are done." He wasn't sure how they could hear him through the noise.

Nymphs' hearing was not much better than a human's, but they seemed not to have any trouble.

"We still have a lot of work to do. Do you have any allergies or foods that you won't eat?"

They waited just long enough for him to shake his head before they navigated their way to the bar. They seemed able to slip into the tight spaces between people as if by magic, but he knew it was a skill nymphs picked up growing up in forests.

Len looked back at his notes. The organization was funding a fairly standard ecological study measuring the environmental impact of the magical communities on the surrounding area. What they were measuring was fairly basic, but the organization had been adamant about opening the study up in Ember. He wasn't sure what they were hoping to find in the wealth of data, but he understood why it had been so important for them to get started in a town like this.

He glanced briefly at the wolves still engaged with their darts and beer, and realized why they had never sent him here to try and persuade the community to agree to participate. *Only, why had they sent him now?*

Birk sat down with two glasses in their hands. "It's sparkling water. I don't tolerate alcohol well, and I figured it was best not to drink while working anyway."

"Thanks," he said, the words getting caught in his throat. He wasn't usually tongue-tied while out on business, but he still hadn't quite settled into his normal routine.

"Rocko said he is cooking up something special for

us, and it will be out here shortly. Should we get to work while we are waiting?"

"Yes, let's get started. As I mentioned, the company has some questions about your latest readings and some of the summaries you provided. I'm here to talk it through with you and report back to them. Sometimes they find that a more informal conversation can lead to observations that may not have made it into the report."

"It sounds like they are looking for something specific. What is it?"

"Honestly, I've been with them a decade now and I still don't know."

"I guess that makes sense. They wouldn't want your bias to seep into the interviews."

Sure, that must be it. It couldn't be that I am just a tool, one too dependent on them to ever leave.

Len glanced around as he walked back to his car. The parking lot was still full, despite the late hour. The meeting had taken longer than expected. Everyone seemed to know Birk and was curious about the new werewolf in town. Thankfully, the other wolves had cleared out when a young female alpha had come in to call them home. It had to have been about him, but the alpha had left him alone, with nothing more than a concerned glance in his direction when his fear had spiked.

The rest of the evening had been more peaceful. And his stomach was still satisfied from the meal that Rocko had brought out for them. Who would have thought there would be a rock troll who owned a bar, or a silkie working behind the counter? Ember was nothing that Len could have imagined, even given all his travels. He could see why so many creatures stayed here, especially with the council that Birk had explained to him. If he were in a different place in his life—and if there wasn't already a wolf pack here—he could imagine settling in a town exactly like this.

Before he realized that he had stopped paying attention to his surroundings, he found himself back at his car. He scanned the area thoroughly, even looking and smelling under his vehicle. Everything seemed safe, so he unlocked the car, set his briefcase down, and started the vehicle. He typed the hotel address into the car's GPS and headed out of the parking lot. He should still be able to get a few hours of sleep before meeting his flight out tomorrow afternoon.

As he drove, Len spotted people still walking around the downtown area. It was evident that Halloween, or Samhain, was a big deal in this town, unless the coffee shop and other businesses usually catered to the more nocturnal crowd.

Less than two minutes later, Len was turning, and there in front of him was his home for the evening. The Hive was an unusual name for a hotel, but he had never had any difficulty with the organization's choices in lodging, so he didn't give it much thought as he reparked his car, picked up his briefcase, and pulled his suitcase out of the trunk. He could have walked.

The hotel was the size of a large home, with just two stories. The parking lot only had a scattering of vehicles, one of which was a white sedan. His fear started to spike. *You are just making it up. It's all in your head. No one is out to harm you.*

It didn't help.

However, he was tired and even he knew that logically there were an abundance of white sedans in the world, and it would probably have been more weird if there hadn't been one in the parking lot. Holding on to that logic, he approached the hotel.

The front doors were made from solid wood and led into a small mudroom where there was space for wet coats and footwear in the colder season. Beyond that was the front desk, where a witch was working behind the counter.

"Hello, I have a reservation for Lennon Smith. You were hopefully told that I would be a late check-in." He hated that the human world put such an emphasis on last names. He had lost his pack name when he had lost his pack. The corporation had dubbed him a Smith for his human ID.

"Welcome, Lennon. I have your information right here, as well as your room key."

A small smile crept to his face when she omitted his last name. If she had familiarity with the local wolf pack, then she must have known that it was a throw-away. Witches didn't typically know much about wolf pack customs, so there were benefits to having magical communities living near each other. Usually, only wanderers, such as himself, really had a grasp of the differences in magical communities' cultures.

A faint buzzing noise came from the side of the desk, and he spied a pixie, dressed in the same jean jacket, short haircut, and jean pants as the ones in the bar. This one carried a cloth and was wiping down all the surfaces in a frantic manner that he could relate to when he became obsessed with a specific activity. They were humming, a high-pitched noise that the witch seemed either used to or unable to hear.

"I've not spent much time around pixies," he said. "They don't typically leave their hive—oh." He stopped short, finally understanding the name of the hotel.

"You will have plenty of experience with them before you leave," the witch said. "They own the hotel."

"They own it?"

"Yep. I'm not sure how many of them there are. They do a lot of the housekeeping and management."

"You can hear them?"

"Not at all. I got the job when I tried applying at Rocko's. She had one of the wolves help translate. I've been working here for months now. They pay well. If they need to tell me anything, I tend to find a note at some point."

"She? I thought pixies were genderless."

"Yes, she, they all are female—at least, that is how they translate their gender to outsiders. If you need anything, feel free to ask away. They are good friends with the alpha's heir."

"Oh." He backed away from the pixie, toward the front desk. The last thing he needed was them reporting back to the local pack about him. He just needed to sleep, then tomorrow he would be out of this town. The next time the company tried to send him here, he would refuse. They must not have realized there was a pack. "I think I will go to my room now. Thank you."

The witch gave a friendly wave goodbye, and Len tried to offer a smile to the pixie who was still fluttering around the front desk.

"Scared. Lonely, scared one," the pixie said. Her voice was high, well past the range most creatures used.

Lennon picked up his suitcase and hurried down a small hallway to a lounging area. He paused, taking a few deep breaths and relaxing his muscles, a skill he had learned in his youth. Once he was back under control, he took stock of the area. His key had the number written on the keychain—205. It was not very safe, but small-town hotels often hadn't made the same changes as the larger chains.

There were signs on the wall pointing to the first-floor rooms, and a large staircase off to the side that led up to where his room would be. A dining area off to the right looked like he would be able to get breakfast before heading out, even if it was something simple. The main area held several couches and armchairs.

Sitting in one of the chairs was a human holding a magazine. The magazine was only covering the lower part of his face, making it easy for Lennon to see that the man was staring straight at him. Most of his frame was hidden by a large wooden support beam, but the face was familiar. He had seen the same man on his trip to St. Louis, and again at the airport. Airports were busy places, and it seemed a coincidence to run into another frequent traveler.

Not here, though. This had to be the man who had been following him in the white sedan.

Len grabbed his suitcase, turned straight around, and raced back to the front desk.

"Excuse me. The human male, how long has he been here?"

"He checked in earlier this evening. Don't worry, we get a lot of humans around here. They come in to do business with the local communities. The same rules apply here as in any public space, so we don't let them know about us."

"This evening? So he is staying for a while?"

"Well, no. He only checked in for one night. Although he did say he might have to extend his stay depending on how his business goes. Is there any trouble?"

"No, no trouble at all. I should head up to bed now. Thank you."

Lennon returned to the common area. The man was no longer there. Taking advantage of his luck, he hurried up the stairs to his room and didn't take another breath until the door had been closed and the deadbolt and security lock had both been put in place.

"No, no, no, no." Len walked over to the small window and went to close the blinds when he saw the secure blackout shutters hidden in the wall paneling. They were often built into hotels that catered to the magical community. He pulled them out and sealed them shut. The window blocked out the outside entirely, giving him a small measure of security.

There was a human following him.

He had felt so paranoid, but the entire time, he had been correct. The organization needed to know about this.

Lennon pulled his briefcase strap over his head, then laid it on the bed. He immediately felt the loss. It often was his armor as he was traveling through busy spaces.

Next, he pulled his phone from one of the front pockets. The battery was low, but he knew from experience that it should be enough to make a call.

He opened his contact list, scrolling through the short selection, until he found Danni. Len started pacing the room as the phone rang. When it went to voicemail, he hung up and dialed again. On the third try, she answered.

"What?"

"It's me, Len … Lennon."

"Yes, I know it's you. I saw your name pop up on the screen. I'm a witch, we sleep at night."

"Oh," he said. "I'm sorry." He glanced at his watch and saw that it was three in the morning, an hour earlier than where Danni was.

"What do you need? This had better be an emergency."

"Yes, it is. I promise. I made it to the hotel in Ember, and there is a human here."

"That is not an emergency. There are humans all over."

"No, no, of course not. It's just that this human has been trailing me. I saw him in St. Louis and at the airport. Someone followed me into town, and now I find him here in the same hotel that I am staying at."

"Doesn't that town only have one hotel?"

"Well, I'm not sure."

"You cannot keep calling me with your paranoid theories, and especially not in the middle of the night— let alone on a ritual night. I'm a witch, and it is Samhain. It's kind of a big deal for us."

"I'm sorry, I forgot. It's just that I am being followed. The human may be trying to get information about the organization. I thought you ought to know."

"Len, I don't know how to say this more clearly. You are not being followed. No one is out to get you."

He plopped down on the chair—a typical hotel chair with wooden arms and very little padding. It was next to a small round wooden table that he put his elbows on, leaning his head on his hands as he continued to talk.

"I am. I am not making this up. I saw him. He was in the lobby reading a magazine, waiting for me to arrive from my meeting. He followed me from the airport. He may have been following me for months."

"This is a pattern," she said. "I am starting to get concerned. First, you call up claiming that you lost your wallet when you forgot it at the hotel. Then someone stole your car when you forgot where you parked it. We excused these things. We try to be understanding about your disabilities. However, you claimed the FBI was following you, trying to bring to light the truth about magical creatures. Now it is some random human stalking you?"

"He could be the FBI."

A deep sigh issued from the other side of the phone, followed by silence, and he knew that he had finally pushed things too far. He would be fired, and left with nothing. He had no home and no pack. Len wasn't built to be a lone wolf, and the organization had been the only thing that had kept him moving forward. Now he would lose that also.

"There has been a change of plans," Danni said.

Len braced himself for his world to shatter down around him.

"You are going to stay in Ember for a while longer. There are some more things that the organization wants to understand. I'm sure you are aware that it is a unique town."

"Oh." It was all that he could manage to say. It wasn't the news he had been bracing himself for.

"I was going to call you in the morning before you headed to the airport, but you have a meeting set with the leader of the local vampire horde."

"Do I need to head over now?" The thought of leaving his room was not something that he even wanted to contemplate.

"They will expect you mid-morning at their main base, which they call the Ranch."

"Morning, but the sun will be out. How will they be able to meet?"

"That is why you will need to go to them. Their leader doesn't require much sleep."

"She is older than …? I mean … I know it isn't polite for outsiders to talk about a vampire's age."

"See that you remember all the rules. I know you don't visit with vampires often, but you must maintain her trust. The leader, Elizabeth, is also head of the Ember council and has enough influence that our study could be discontinued."

"I'll head to the airport after I meet with the vampires?"

"No. Your ticket has been cancelled, and your hotel room will be extended. Right now, you will stay in Ember until you are needed elsewhere."

"There are werewolves here," Len said.

"They have been made aware of your presence and have not objected."

"What about the human?"

"You are a werewolf. If the human becomes a problem, eat him."

"I don't … I would never … we don't actually—" But before he could produce a coherent sentence, the call ended.

They wanted him to stay in this town with a human who was stalking him and a werewolf pack of which he had already made one member angry enough to storm out of a room. He needed to go, now, tonight. He tucked his phone back in the pocket of his briefcase and picked it up. Grabbing the handle of his suitcase, he turned to the door, and then froze.

The human could be right outside the door. Len put his eye up to the security hole. The hallway was empty, but that didn't mean anything. There was only a very limited view. Or, what if he was waiting back in the lobby, or next to his car?

If he left, where would he go? The corporation had dictated his actions for the last decade. Everything he owned was in the suitcase and the briefcase. Sure, there was money, probably a fair bit of it, since his paychecks got deposited and, besides an amount that went to his mother, were never touched. There was no need, when the organization paid for nearly everything. But that was just money. It wasn't family, and Len wouldn't make it as a lone wolf.

He threw his briefcase down on the chair and let go of his suitcase. There wasn't a choice, really. He could stay in this town, and if the wolves decided to run him out, well, he wasn't planning on staying very long anyway.

CHAPTER
FIVE

Lennon waited until the sun started peeking through the curtains before he climbed out of bed. It was a soft bed, with a thick blanket that had enveloped him throughout the night. As far as hotel beds went, it was one of the nicest. It was the kind of bed he would want to use each night, if he'd had a place of his own.

And the experience had been wasted. He hasn't slept much more than a few hours, and even then, his dreams had been haunted. The comforter had come completely untucked as he had pulled at it in his sleep. The sheets looked more like a braided breadstick than quality linen.

He opened his suitcase on the luggage rack and studied his options. Most of the clothes were tucked in the side with a plastic covering, his version of a dirty clothes hamper. He should have done laundry before he'd left St. Louis, but there had never seemed to be time. Thankfully, he still had a few more days before he would run out completely. Maybe his next assignment would allow him time to find a Laundromat.

Len pulled out a pair of khaki pants, and after being unable to locate an ironing board, put them on the bed with a towel underneath, before pulling out his travel iron and pressing until all the wrinkles were out. Over the years, he had become quite adept at rolling his clothes so they took up less space and were not too travel worn, but on important occasions, he made sure to take the time to be extra polished.

Next, he pulled out one of his button-down shirts, a light blue one that he took his time ironing any last wrinkles out of. He wasn't in a hurry this morning, as there were still a few hours until his meeting with the vampires. He should probably go downstairs and get some breakfast, or at least some coffee, but he wasn't that brave. Even if the human following him was all in his head, like Danni believed, he still didn't want to take that chance. Except it wasn't all in his head. He *knew* it wasn't all in his head.

Once his clothes were ready, he took a shower, grateful that the hotel provided little shampoos and conditioners. He had left his in the last hotel, again. Clean and dressed, he pulled out his laptop and looked at the notes that had been sent for the meeting.

The file on the vampires was more detailed than Lennon was used to. There were pictures of the Ranch, with aerial photos showing the main house as well as the gated community built around it. There were also photos of key vampires he was likely to meet, including Elizabeth, who physically appeared to be eight years old and whose age was indicated with just the word "old."

Len had long suspected that the organization was run by a vampire, a very old vampire who had an intense interest in the magical sciences, and generations of accumulated wealth to spend on it. However, he had not done anything more than speculate, for fear of putting his job at risk.

His phone let out a loud, piercing noise, a notification from his calendar telling him that it was time to go. After being late one too many times, Danni had taken over his schedule, making sure to set reminders for him. It wasn't that he didn't try to be organized. It was just that he tended to get distracted and then forgot completely.

A second notification prompted him that it really was time to go. He searched for his wallet, sifting through the discarded clothes from the night before, then rummaging through his briefcase, and finally found it on the back of the toilet.

"It's always the last place you look." Len put his hand on the doorknob, peeking through the security hole. There was a pixie fluttering up and down, an abandoned cleaning cart in the center of the hallway.

"Maybe I should have been a pixie instead of a werewolf." He straightened. "Okay, no more stalling." He wondered what Danni would think if she knew that he talked to himself like this. She would probably add it to his file as one more way that he wasn't quite measuring up.

"You can be a pixie, a pixie, a pixie … the hive will

let you join us … but no worries … the one that caused you fear is not inside."

The words flittered through the door in a high-pitched ringing. The pixie wasn't even looking in his direction. She didn't seem to be moving at all. One second she was holding a pile of towels, and the next she was dumping dirty laundry into a bin.

"Note to self," he mumbled, "the pixies can hear you." But at least she had let him know that the human wasn't around. It gave him enough courage to turn the handle and leave the safety of his room.

"Thank you," he said to the pixie as he passed her in the hallway.

On a plane several years ago, he had read a magazine article about quantum mechanics, about how things can be in two places at the same time. He wondered if somehow that applied to these creatures. They didn't quite seem in sync with the rest of reality.

"Maybe they are a glitch in the matrix," he said as he walked down the stairs.

"Matrix … movie about being stuck in a computer program," the pixie above him said.

"Vernacular … meaning something is out of the ordinary," a pixie in the dining area said.

"Joke … sarcasm … not literal," another voice said from the direction of the front desk.

A low hum seemed to fill the hotel. It wasn't spoken language, but he could hear it resonating, and once he was able to place it, he realized that the hotel had been full of the same humming the night before. He had just been too worried to pay attention to it.

He would have to put a call in to Danni. If the company expected him to stay in this town, they would have to find him a new hotel. He would never be able to unhear the buzzing again.

Len paused at the end of the staircase. The downstairs area seemed empty of the human, but he was afraid that he might be waiting for Len through the front door. He pivoted, going to the back of the stairs, and found a back door tucked next to an elevator in the corner. Taking one last look around to make sure he was alone, he slipped outside.

It opened into a small outdoor patio that had a thin covering of snow. The air was crisp and clean, the way it is in elevations above the city smog, especially with most of the pollutants trapped in the frozen moisture. Except there was a brief hit of the human in the air, a faint combination of sweet stench and French fries, as if he had been back here.

An awning hanging off the hotel sheltered an outdoor table and chairs. The seats were dry, and the man very well could have sat out here eating his breakfast earlier in the morning. It would be perfectly normal behavior for a human. That didn't stop Len's heart from pounding, and the adrenaline coursing through his body.

He needed to walk around the side of the hotel to get to his car, so he could make his meeting. So, Len took a few tentative steps toward the side of the building and moved his body close to the brick so he could peer around the corner. There was the human standing on the sidewalk. He held something black and large in his hand, pointing up into the air. He was talking and showing off another object in his other hand. Len didn't take the time to process what he was seeing. He turned around and bolted in the opposite direction, maneuvering around the outdoor furniture and leaping over a small rock wall to the back of several connected retail buildings. He ran full out, searching for a break, before spotting a small alley.

Len took the corner at full speed until he was on the sidewalk. He didn't stop, just continued running. There was no thought or plan in his head. He just had to get someplace safe. He didn't even realize that people were out walking until he ran solidly into one.

Hands gripped Len's arms, holding him in place. He jerked away, trying to escape the grip, but the arms wrapped around him, squeezing his chest with just enough pressure to feel snug but not painful. He kept fighting until his body relaxed, finally recognizing the scent of wolf … safety … home. He collapsed into the arms, tears falling freely down his face, as his body cast off all the stress of the last few days.

Len didn't know how long he stayed there, in broad daylight, being held by a stranger. Slowly, he came back to himself. Arms were still snugly wrapped around him, but their bodies sat on the ground now, the other person slightly rocking and whispering, "It's okay. I've got you. You're going to be okay now."

The voice was melodic, and he found himself closing his eyes for a few moments to enjoy listening to it. However, his heartbeat was slower now. The other wolf would know that he was calming down. Len looked up and saw the light brown eyes, tanned skin, and messy hair of the man who had been glaring at him the night before.

Len jerked away; this time, the stranger released him. He clambered to his feet and noticed his briefcase lying on the sidewalk, smeared with dirt.

"Excuse me," he said, grabbing his briefcase and hurriedly brushing it off. "I'm late for a meeting and need to be on my way."

"Wait."

The man wasn't an alpha. Len didn't have to obey his order, but he was still a visitor in this space.

"I'm Ancel."

Ancel held out his hand, and the professionalism of the moment comforted Len. It was just another business relationship.

"I'm Len … Lennon. I am in town briefly for some business." He reached out and grabbed the other man's hand. The handshake was firm, less a power play and more a showcase of natural strength.

Ancel wasn't exceptionally tall, at least compared to Len, who was a few inches over six feet, but he was dressed in a simple black T-shirt that clung to his frame, showing off some definition. He was an attractive man, but Len worked to control his interest. It had been too many years since he had been around wolves, and he was out of practice. The best thing to do would be to retreat.

"It was a pleasure to meet you," Len said. "Thank you for the assistance, but as I mentioned, I need to go." He turned and walked away, trying to escape the natural musk of the other wolf. Except it followed him as he walked, along with another set of footsteps. He stopped, turning around, and the other wolf was right behind him.

"Lennon, wait. What happened? What's wrong?"

The way his name rolled off of Ancel's tongue caused his stomach to flutter. It was a sharp contrast from the distain he usually felt when mentioned by business associates. He hated his full name. He hated that he couldn't live up to it. By the time he'd had his naming ceremony, he and the pack had all known he was gay. Being given a name meaning "lover" had been cruel. Especially when he had only wanted to be loved. So he had shortened it to Len: "to be brave." He'd known he would need to be brave when he'd walked out of his pack.

"Are you okay?" Ancel asked.

"I'm late for a meeting. I am supposed to be at the vampire's Ranch right now."

"You're scared of vampires?"

Len paused, confused. "No."

"Then what was that? You were petrified, and now you are trying to brush it off like nothing happened."

He imagined breaking down and telling this man that he was so scared of a human that he had fled, panicked, right into his arms. "I would rather not talk about it."

They stood staring at each other for a few heartbeats before Ancel broke the silence. "Fine. Which way is your car?"

"Why?"

"You don't have to talk about what scared you, but you are a visitor in my territory, and I will make sure you arrive safely for your meeting."

Len gave him another glance. He wasn't an alpha—he couldn't be. Alphas had an energy that bled off of them, making them undeniable. Ancel wasn't like that. He was a caretaker.

"My car is back at the hotel. I'm headed there now. I must have gotten turned around. I'm sorry if I caused you any discomfort."

He started walking, the other wolf keeping pace beside him. Part of him felt comforted by the wolf's presence. Ancel looked like he knew how to protect himself, and if the human was still around, then they would both be able to handle him. However, another part of him wanted Ancel far away.

It wasn't that Len hadn't had relationships since he had left the pack. They had just all been with humans, brief one-night stands or week-long romances that had ended when he'd left again. None of them had been with another wolf who could sense his desire.

They walked in silence back to the hotel, where he pressed the unlock button on his keys so he could find his newest rental car, trying not to let Ancel see him scanning for signs of the human.

"This is me. I do need to be going."

Ancel stared at him intently for a moment. When Len's heartbeat started to rise, Ancel took a step back. "If you need anything, the alpha here will help."

Len's face flushed, and his hands started shaking.

"I'm good. I won't be in town long." He slipped into the car, starting it as fast as he could, and left the parking lot without even looking where he was supposed to be going. He had to pull over to plug in the address for the vampire's den. Before he took off again, he relaxed a little at the sight of the empty road.

The drive was short, just off the main part of town, and his thoughts filtered back to the feeling of Ancel's arms around him. Once he saw the large metal gate that marked the entrance to the vampire territory, he tried to clear his mind of the wolf and focus on the business at hand, but it was hard. Then the gates started to open before he could let anyone know he had arrived.

"Great. I'm expected."

He drove through a subdivision with perfectly manicured lawns and empty driveways. It was straight out of a horror movie. As he approached the giant mansion in the distance, the houses started to look more lived in. Some people were walking around outside in the daylight, some vehicles were parked on the road, and a few children were playing. Although the houses still looked a little too perfect to be real.

The road led through a large lawn that could have easily been mistaken for a park. When he reached the end, there was a turnaround like he had only seen in movies. He looked around, hoping to find a side entrance, or at least somewhere less intimidating to leave his car.

Resigned, he parked the car with enough space to easily allow another car to drive around him, and headed to the entrance. He climbed the steps until he reached a set of double doors. Len lifted his hand to knock and then thought better of it. He searched around for a doorbell and finally settled on using the knocker shaped like a lion.

The knock echoed in his ears. Len straightened his tie and made sure his pants were straight. As the door remained unanswered, he started looking around, trying to find another entrance. Columns obstructed his view of the side, so he looked up. Every window was sealed off to make sure that sunlight did not creep past.

"This has to be a mistake," Len said. "It's daylight, for goodness' sake." He pulled up his phone and was opening Danni's text messages when the door opened.

The entryway was shadowed, with only the daylight allowing Len to see the man dressed in a white shirt, a black vest, and a black bowtie.

Len hesitated, the reality of walking into a vampire's den finally dawning on him. Sure, vampires didn't find werewolves tasty, but it didn't make this any smarter of an idea.

"You are expected," the butler said.

Len straightened, fixed his tie again, and strode

through the door. The butler shut it, leaving a dim light on the ceiling that seemed enough for the butler to find his way to a second set of doors. Len followed the man through and into an entryway that was several stories high. Right in front of him was a staircase leading to the second floor. It was a deep brown that had been polished with time as much as oil. The walls were adorned with pictures painted in a variety of styles. He didn't recognize any of them. As he took it all in, he saw a large chandelier hanging above the room, its crystals reflecting the light and drawing his attention.

"The mistress is waiting for you. This way."

He pulled his attention away from the room and tried to attend to the reason he was here. *Focus, focus, focus,* he chanted to himself as he followed the man down a hallway hidden by the stairs. He was led into a sitting room covered in white wallpaper and white carpet. There were two couches and a chair, all framed in a light wood with white upholstery on them. They looked like they would break if he sat on them.

"They will be with you shortly," the butler said. He was gone before Len could tear his eyes away from the glare long enough to answer.

Carefully, he sat on the edge of one of the couches, placing his briefcase on a white marble coffee table. As he started to pull out his tablet and electronic pen, he noticed the table base was textured. At first, it looked like white waves peeking out from the thick base, but as he looked closer, he noticed that they were human skulls. His adrenaline spiked, and he had to fight down the urge to run. He had a job to do, after all.

"It's a private joke."

The voice was soft and high-pitched like a child's. Len stood and turned to face the speaker and saw a small girl dressed in a bright pink dress, with a bow in her hair.

"Mistress Elizabeth," Len said.

The girl giggled. Then, her smile dropped and her cheeks relaxed, transforming her into a woman older than her body would suggest. She focused on Len as if reading his very soul. He stood there, quietly, letting her take stock of him as he kept his eyes averted, a wolf behavior, but one she should recognize.

"It seems that they briefed you well." She walked over to the chair and pulled herself up into the seat with little effort, despite it being almost to her chest. Then she sat down on the arm of the chair, her own arms folded and her legs tucked underneath.

Len couldn't help the chuckle that came out of him, but at her stern glance, pivoted to clearing his throat.

"The organization asked me to meet with you today to discuss their current conservation efforts in Ember and answer any questions that you may have."

He waited, hoping for some sort of acknowledgement, but she just sat there, unmoving. She had stopped even the pretense of breathing. His mind emptied, and he started to panic. He was normally so much better with people—but then, she wasn't a person. As he opened his mouth to say something—anything—two men entered the room.

"You're late," Elizabeth said.

"I'm sorry. I lost track of time." The man who had

spoken was dressed in a vest and suit pants not unlike Len's. The other wore a simple brown plaid dress shirt and a pair of jeans. They held hands as they sat down on the opposite couch.

"We will talk about this later, after our business has been completed. This is Jeffery, my daytime assistant, and this is his mate Lucas."

Mate—as in, together in a relationship ...

"That is correct," Jeffery said. He had a short edge to his voice, and Len realized that he must have said that aloud.

"I apologize," he said. Len tried to come up with something more to say, but he kept looking at the way their fingers were joined and how relaxed they were sitting next to each other. They were together—in the open, and no one seemed to care otherwise. He thought about sitting next to Ancel, their fingers laced together, while the rest of the world continued as if it were nothing.

"Now, I believe you were going to introduce yourself," Elizabeth said.

"Yes, I'm sorry. I am Len ... Lennon. I work with the organization ..."

"What organization would that be?" Jeffery asked.

"Yes, excuse me. I work for Eternal Beauty Environmental Protection. It is a non-profit that funds conservation efforts in magical communities."

"Why do you call it 'the organization'?" Lucas asked. "Birk calls it that as well."

His voice was a bit lower than Jeffery's, and less

harsh, and he seemed less jaded by the years. By the modern attire, Len speculated that he had probably been turned within the decade.

"You know Birk?" Len asked. But then, why wouldn't they know each other? With so many magical communities living beside each other, they were liable to interact more than anywhere else. "I suppose it has become vernacular, since EBEP doesn't exactly roll off the tongue. To be honest, it was called that long before I joined, and I never thought to question it."

"How much do you know about this corporation?" Elizabeth asked.

He faced her as he answered. "I've worked with them for a decade. During that time, I have visited countless sites where we are doing great work on improving the ecological foundation of the magical species, working to preserve it for the next generation."

"All that time without a pack," she said.

The words hit Lennon harder than he expected. His throat started to close, and his eyes began to water. He tried to ignore it, bringing back his professional persona, but everything was so raw. He sat blinking away tears for a few seconds before he could continue.

"The organization is my pack. That is why I am so happy to be here helping to continue their good work." It sounded like complete garbage to his ears, and from the slight frown on the vampire mistress's face, he knew she thought so as well. He couldn't help glancing over at the two men, who were looking at him with open curiosity. At least it was better than pity.

"How much do you know about the origins of the corporation?" Elizabeth asked.

"The organization has been around for many years and has worked on countless projects. One of the reasons we have been able to keep our homelands from the encroaching human population is because of the good work of the organization," he said, turning to face Elizabeth again.

"So they haven't told you the specifics, I see. Do you know who founded it? Do you even know who runs it now?"

"I …" No one had cared so much before. They had been happy to take the benefits the organization had offered, and not ask too many questions. Len was the same way. They had given him a purpose and a community. All they'd asked was that he not pry too much into what was happening.

"I see," Elizabeth said. "But you have an idea, don't you? Something that you have pieced together from all the small bits of information they have given you over the years. You remind me of Phoenix. Not exactly, but there is a similarity about you."

Len shifted slightly on the couch, but stopped as soon as he felt it move beneath him. "I don't know who that is."

"I think it's about time to change that. I believe I understand why they sent you to me."

"I am here to answer any questions you may have about the ongoing conservation efforts in Ember. The organization wants to make sure they maintain the full support of your council, and as head of the council, your opinion carries weight with the other members."

She smiled at him, a knowing smile, and Len felt certain that the organization was run by a vampire, and one that Elizabeth was intimately familiar with.

"Excuse me, mistress."

Len jumped at the interruption. The butler stood in the doorway, his eyes cast downward. While he was perfectly poised, Len got the impression he wanted to be anywhere but here.

"Security asked me to come and get you," the butler said. "They said it was of the utmost importance."

Elizabeth frowned slightly, then jumped down from the chair. She was at the door before the butler had even finished speaking. She gave a subtle nod, and Jeffery untangled his fingers from Lucas before following behind her.

The room seemed to collapse in with their loss, the unbroken whiteness of the space overwhelming. Len could feel Lucas on the other couch, his gaze focused on him. He tried to ignore it, picking up his tablet and reading back through his notes. The tension built, and finally, Len glanced up at the vampire. There was a smile on his face, one that curled higher on one side, as if to tell the other person that you thought they were contemptible. Len's eyes immediately jumped to the shine of the wallpaper. The brightness caused a small headache.

The entire time, he felt the stare of the vampire on him.

Vampires don't think about eye contact the same way as wolves, he reminded himself. But he couldn't bring himself to look Lucas in the eye.

"You mentioned that you know Birk?" Len said. He couldn't take the silence anymore, or the disdain radiating off the other man. The words weren't planned. They came out without thought, a reaction to the stress.

"Yes, we met shortly after I was turned."

Len took that in, but it didn't help him to determine the vampire's age. Nymphs tended to live centuries, and they also remained ageless.

"Was that long ago?" He regretted the question as soon as he said it. It was too close to asking the vampire his age. "I mean, do you know them well?"

"Not as well as I would like. I am still under restrictions and not allowed to leave the Ranch. Birk visits occasionally, more so now that they are involved in this project. I enjoy their company when they come. We have plenty of time to continue to build our friendship."

The last line was spoken as if eternity was still a mystery instead of a burden, and Len was sure that Lucas was quite young. Maybe even a fledgling, barely created, and not allowed in the presence of others without supervision. Yet they were here, alone, in this room. Len picked up his tablet again, not even bothering to read, just using it as a moment to collect his thoughts and push the anxiety away.

It only took a few seconds for logic to return. The vampires would not have left them alone if Lucas were unsafe. Even if he lost control, all Len would need to do was yell, and there were probably hundreds of Lucas's peers to help restrain him. This last thought was less comforting, but Len was a wolf, and vampires did not—could not—feed on wolves.

"So, you and Jeffery are in a relationship?" Len asked. As soon as the words left his mouth, he wished he could snatch them back. Lucas tensed, and his smile disappeared.

"Yes."

"The vampires don't have a problem with that?" He hadn't meant to say the words out loud, but his brain kept acting on its own. Right now, he couldn't think about anything else but seeing two men happily together in front of him.

"Should they?"

"No, but some humans care, and vampires come from humans … and werewolves care a lot."

At the words, Lucas shifted slightly. His hands opened up, and his legs spread. Something Len had said had made him less of a threat to the vampire.

"I came to Ember as a human," Lucas said. "I didn't know that I was vampire kin, just that my parents were from here and I needed to start over. My ex-husband wasn't thrilled to find out he was married to a man. It wasn't my choice to be a vampire, but things have worked out well for me. I have found a family and a man that I love. I'm sorry that your family refused to love you for all of who you are."

He knows. Len tried to think back and figure out when he had tipped his hand, but then, when you have experienced the loss of everything, for just existing, you begin to recognize it in others. He felt his eyes start to water, and he closed them to try to stop the flood of emotions. *This is a business meeting, dammit.*

"There is a pack of wolves here that would take you in," Lucas said.

Len stood. Before he knew it, he was behind the couch. There wasn't much room between it and the wall, but he stood there, using it as armor. He was flooded with a mix of emotions. The fear that always came when thinking about his pack—his old pack—but also the memory of Ancel's arms around him.

"I'm sorry," Lucas said. "I didn't mean to upset you."

His heart was racing, and the vampire most likely could hear each beat pounding inside his chest. He focused on calming himself down, and gradually his heartbeat returned to normal. Len moved back to the couch and picked up his tablet like nothing had happened. The two sat in silence, neither seemingly willing to start the conversation back up.

"Excuse me, sir. The mistress has asked for you to join her." The butler was again in the doorway. He seemed annoyed at having to come back, although maybe that was Len reading too much into his slight frown.

He waited, expecting Lucas to stand up and follow the human, leaving Len alone. When Lucas didn't move, Len realized that the butler had been addressing him.

"Yes, of course," he said, rising from the couch again.

He followed the butler through a winding maze of hallways. Lucas had joined them as well, and Len felt boxed in, as if they were concerned about him wandering off.

As if anyone would want to go wandering through a mansion full of vampires.

Eventually, they were led into a room full of monitors. They looked like a rendition of a lackluster reality TV show. Most of the screens showed rows of empty streets, but right in the middle, on the largest monitor, there was the human.

L en froze. His eyes drank in the sight that his mind was trying to catch up to. A smaller monitor showed an abandoned white sedan by the gates. There was a piece of clothing hanging over the top of the fencing to cover the spikes. The human must have put it there to climb over. It didn't seem effective, more like something that someone in a movie would do.

The human was now wandering in the middle of the vampire subdivision. He was holding up something small and black. Len moved closer to the monitor, trying to focus on the object, until he realized it was a camera. The human's mouth was moving as he moved the camera around, occasionally turning it back on himself. He was putting on a show … for someone.

"Do you know him?" Elizabeth asked.

"He's been following me," Len said. "I saw him in the last city I was in. Then I saw him at the airport in Denver. I didn't think much of it until he showed up here. I've seen him a few times over the months, usually in crowded spaces. I thought he was another frequent traveler. I don't know who he is or what he wants. He won't seem to go away. He's … well, I'm not sure, but in my gut I know he is trouble."

The goosebumps on his arms started to rise, and he flushed as he looked at the human. It hit him then: Len was in a room surrounded by vampires, but the only thing that scared him was the human on the screen.

"That sounds a bit … paranoid," Elizabeth said.

The words didn't surprise him, but they did hurt to hear. Why would no one believe him? Len turned toward the vampire mistress. "Are you in direct contact with the organization? They think I am paranoid, but I'm not. He is a real threat. The human could expose everything, and no one is taking him seriously."

Elizabeth stared at him, her expression impassive.

"What have they done to you that causes you to be scared of a human?" she asked.

He wanted to argue with her, to explain that this wasn't just any human. There was something about him that needed to be taken seriously. But he couldn't. Instead, he was flooded with self-doubt. If everyone thought you were paranoid—well, then maybe you were.

The vampire mistress turned away from Len, facing the screens. She made a gesture, and one of the vampires picked up a walkie-talkie and spoke into it. "You are good to go."

Suddenly, the room started to close in on him. There were vampires everywhere, and Len couldn't move without finding himself next to one of them. He needed to leave, to run, to escape.

He felt a hand on his shoulder, squeezing firmly enough to ground him to the moment. Len looked up and saw Lucas, who gave a curt nod before stepping back. All the vampires had seemed to shift slightly, giving him room where there had been none before. Len took one last breath to steady himself and then turned to the screen.

A group of fifteen vampire kin—humans that had the genetic predisposition to be turned into vampires—showed up on the monitor. They were all dressed in black suits, and they moved like humans—since, for all intents and purposes, they were, unless they chose to be changed—although ones trained to protect.

The human's white shirt stood out on the screen. Len expected him to run, but instead he just held up his camera, filming as he was approached. The security moved closer, and he put his hand in his pocket, pulling out a small bag. It looked like a cloth bag made to hold dice. The human put one hand in the bag and started flinging out the contents onto the men, all the while filming on a wobbly camera.

"Is that … salt?" Len asked.

The security paused their approach, cautiously watching the human.

"Why aren't they doing anything?" Len asked.

Jeffery moved over to Len, standing next to him, and his hand moved to his arm. He wasn't sure if it was meant to comfort him or threaten him, but Len took it as a demand and tried to watch the screen in silence.

At once, the human abandoned the bag, letting it drop to the ground, and reached to his back pocket, where he pulled out a metallic cross. It gleamed in the sunlight, reflecting the sun into bright spots that were redirected onto the kin. They stood impassive, not even flinching as the light was reflected into their eyes. Fury started to build in Len at their impassivity. They had a chance to end it all, and the human had played them like puppets. He started rushing toward the security detail, the cross held up in front of him. The kin still didn't move, didn't react, just watched him as he went.

Finally, Len couldn't take it anymore. "Why aren't they doing anything?"

"Why?" Jeffery said. "He is harmless. If they wait him out, he will post his video, and nothing will come of it. If they fight back, then there will be a story. Next thing we know, we have more humans here. There will be police investigating. It will be a bigger risk of exposure. Security isn't in any danger, and they are doing exactly what they are supposed to do."

On the screen, the human raised his hands into the air and screamed something at the kin. He broke out in a massive grin, like he had won something, and then turned back to climb over the wall, but as he retreated, the iron gates opened and the human waltzed out. The camera followed him back to his car, parked right outside the gates. They watched as he got in, started it, and drove away.

As soon as the car began moving, Elizabeth turned from the screens, as if they were completely forgotten. "Well, I suppose we should finish our meeting."

Elizabeth was back sitting on the chair. Jeffery and Lucas were again on the couch, their fingers entwined. Len stood pacing near the doorway. He had tried to sit down, but had lasted less than a second before he'd jumped up again. The vampires seemed completely at ease watching him with expressionless faces. He couldn't bring his body back under control, his mind racing, replaying what had happened with the human over and over again.

Security had done nothing, and the human had walked away without causing any harm. It was clear watching the man interact with trained professionals that he wasn't the FBI or any sort of agency out to discover the magical community. He was someone who had watched too many horror movies. Most likely, he was a conspiracy theorist, and while he had discovered some aspect of their world, his actions proved he wasn't a threat. Danni had been right—Len had been paranoid.

He sat back down on the couch, but he hadn't

settled yet. His legs kept bouncing, and his hands were clasped tightly. It all logically made sense, but he couldn't let go of his gut feeling that the human was nothing but trouble.

"Why were you kicked out of your pack?" Elizabeth asked.

The suddenness of the question catapulted Len back into the present. "I wasn't. I left on my own."

"It is very apparent that you are not a lone wolf," Elizabeth said. "You need people. You hold tight to their company as if it is the air you need to breathe. If you left on your own, you did so for a reason."

Len couldn't help the glance he gave Jeffery and Lucas, the longing transparent on his face, though he couldn't say the words aloud.

"Ah," Elizabeth said.

"I am here to talk to you about the ongoing conservation efforts that are happening in Ember." He grasped on to this thought, trying to turn this meeting back into something that he understood. Len knew business. He had spent the last decade making it the only consistent aspect of himself.

"When was the last time that you let out your wolf?" Jeffery asked.

"I …" He didn't intend to answer the question. It was none of the vampire's concern. Except, he didn't remember. There were so few opportunities when he was constantly in new territories.

"It's settled, then. You will go meet with the wolves." Elizabeth turned to Jeffery, who pulled out his phone and started typing.

"No," Len said. "I am here to talk about the ongoing conservation project happening at Ember. Since that is no longer on the agenda, I think it is best that I take my leave." He reached for his tablet, slid it back into his briefcase, and stood, carrying his items to the doorway. "Thank you for helping with the human. If I can be of assistance with the project, then please feel free to reach out."

"Stop," Elizabeth said. Her voice resonated with the authority of an alpha.

Len paused, trying to reason in his head why he should keep walking, but it was too ingrained in his very essence to listen.

"Sit back down," she said. When Len still resisted, she added, "Now!"

He turned around and sat back on the couch. He stayed on the edge, his briefcase still in his hands. His lip curled up, and he let out a low snarl, like a pup trying to show his displeasure when they both knew he could do nothing else.

"Why won't you go to your own kind?" Elizabeth asked.

Len was taken aback at the question. He'd expected a command—that Elizabeth would tell him exactly what he would do next. Instead, she sat on the arm of the chair, her attention focused on him, waiting for an answer.

"Wolves are not vampires," he said. His words felt stuck and disconnected. He didn't want to talk about his past, but the mistress had not left him with a way to avoid that option. "They are more rigid in their expectations. Maybe we have too much humanity coursing through our blood. We also can't hide who we are. When you are attracted to someone, everyone knows. As long as everyone acts respectfully, it usually isn't a problem. Your senses will tell you if the emotions are reciprocated or not, and wolves act accordingly."

"They could tell you were attracted to men," Lucas said. "That is why you were sent away?"

Len nodded his head, a small motion that showed the shame he had built up for who he was.

"Did you ever act inappropriately?" Elizabeth asked.

"No. No one else in my pack felt the same way, and I respected that. But it didn't matter. Knowing I felt that was too much for them."

"Then that won't be a problem," Elizabeth said. "Is everything set?"

He looked around in confusion, but it was Jeffery who answered.

"Phoenix says he is welcome at any time. I'm sending over the pack address now. You should be able to use your GPS to get there."

Len's phone vibrated, and he pulled it out to see a message from an unknown number.

"I think it is best I head back to the hotel for now," he said. "I'm sure I could meet with the pack tomorrow." *Or never.* He stood and walked as quickly as he could toward the doorway.

"You will go and meet with the pack," Elizabeth said. "You will not deviate or put it off. If you do, I will reach out directly to the board of your company, and they will know."

A chill went through Len. It wasn't a threat, but a statement of fact. Elizabeth knew exactly how effective it would be.

The butler appeared as if summoned and gestured for Len to follow him to the door. The sun was bright when he left the house, a sharp contrast to the fluorescent lighting inside. It was still early, and he was startled to realize that he had only been inside a few hours. It had felt so much longer.

He placed his briefcase on the passenger seat and headed to the driver's side, moving slowly, trying to postpone the inevitable. Scenarios of taking the car and driving away flashed in his mind. He could go anywhere, not just where the organization sent him. He could find a place to live and put down roots. Except that each day, he would die slowly. He was not a lone wolf. He would do exactly what was expected of him, even if it broke him in the process.

L en exhaled as the metal gate closed behind him. A part of him still felt connected to the elder vampire, like there was a magical cord that wouldn't let him go until he ended up at the alpha's house. It was all in his head—probably.

His phone was set up to give him directions. It showed that he would arrive in less than ten minutes, which was too quick for him to come to terms with what he had been asked to do.

There had been another pack. His second year working for the corporation, they had sent him to a pack in Northern California. They were funding a restoration project after a massive wildfire had taken out most of the pack lands. The organization had assured him that he would be fine—it was California, after all. The meeting had gone well for the first thirty minutes. At that point, word had gotten around that he had left his pack, and why, and he had been escorted off their property with a warning never to come back. The company had replaced him with a different bureaucrat and had never sent him to another wolf pack again—until now.

Except they hadn't sent him, the vampire had. If he could just appeal to Danni, then she could tell him to go back to the hotel, and everything would turn out all right. He pulled off to the side of the road, the rental car unhappy at being driven on the grassy dirt. Lennon dialed her number and was not surprised when she picked up on the first ring.

"I know what you are going to say." Her voice seemed to echo within the car's interior. "But we think this is a great idea. Keep your appointment with the wolves."

"You remember what happened last time?" he said.

"Yes, but times have changed, and this pack is different."

"What aren't you telling me?"

"Stop thinking that everyone is plotting against you. Meet with the pack. It's time."

The call ended, and his phone flickered back to his lock screen. It was an outdated picture of him and his mother when he had been eight years old. She was laughing, trying to get him to smile for the picture. He was standing there stoically waiting for the moment to be over. *What did she mean "it's time"?*

He could call back. Most likely, she wouldn't answer. She never did when she had put her foot down, and she'd seemed adamant in her declaration. There might as well have been an "or else" tacked on to the end of the conversation.

The fantasy of a house somewhere alone flittered back into his mind. Maybe he would build it deep in the forest. He could stay in Colorado. There was something peaceful about the state.

Instead, he put the car in drive and started following his phone's directions. His mind spun, trying to prepare for the interactions with the wolves and their inevitable rejection. He looked in the rearview mirror out of habit, and there was the white sedan. The human's face was visible through the windshield. He stared straight at Lennon, his mouth moving as if talking to an audience, but he was the only one in the car.

Len's heart rate spiked. His brain went fuzzy. Yet, some part of him, the part that was used to constantly being in a state of panic, kept driving.

He followed the neutral voice that emanated from his phone as it led him past trees and undeveloped land. Then it shifted to subdivisions with houses that were spaced far apart. The address led straight to the alpha's house, which was the largest of them all, built to accommodate the pack's needs.

Len didn't stop. The voice passively told him to make a U-turn as he continued down the road. He randomly turned, then did so again, until he eventually found himself back at the small downtown area.

The white sedan stayed behind him the entire time.

Len looped back to the vampires, even stopping by their gates, hoping to be let in or for security to magically appear. Instead, the human started to get out of his car, and Len stepped on the gas. Unfortunately, the human was quick and was right behind him again.

He kept driving. There wasn't a lot in town. There wasn't even a traffic light, just one four-way stop sign on the main street. So, he kept doing loops with the white sedan following behind him. Nearly an hour passed. Len didn't relax throughout the entire drive. His mind oscillated between fear of the human and chastising himself for being afraid. Then he became concerned that the wolves would call the organization and tell them he hadn't shown up. As he continued driving, he could be losing everything.

Len pulled up to the stop sign yet again. The white sedan was still behind him, pausing at the stop sign as Len drove forward. Only this time, an older woman walked onto the road, moving slowly, a bag balanced on a walker as she crept across the street. The human went to drive his car around her, but suddenly, there was a large man there—Rocko from the bar—who started shouting at the human and held his hand to the roof of the car, gesturing for the woman to keep walking.

This was finally his chance. He turned at the next opportunity. Then he turned again. He did it a few more times until he was alone on a side street tucked behind some trees. He waited long enough to get himself under control and make sure the white sedan hadn't made its way back before he finally started listening to the GPS again and made his way back to the alpha's house.

He pulled into the driveway, sitting in the car with

the engine running. He still didn't trust that the human hadn't found a way to follow him. Len watched, waiting for him to appear down the road. Instead, there was a knock on his passenger window, causing him to jump so high his head hit the roof.

L en pushed the button to roll down the window, then went back to looking out his rearview mirror at the road.

"I'm sorry for startling you," the wolf said. "I'm surprised you didn't hear me."

"I have been focusing on something else."

"The car following you?"

Len studied the wolf. She was of average height with long black hair that was pulled back out of her face. She wore a simple tank top that showcased her muscular build. She knew how to fight.

He realized then that he recognized her. She had been the one to clear the wolves out of the bar at Rocko's.

"How did you know about the car following me?" Len asked.

"I could hear you both passing. I'm sensitive to noise. I figured it was some kids messing around, even though I didn't recognize the cars, but then you pulled in."

"You're the alpha?"

"I'm the heir. You should come in."

"But … what if he comes back?"

"Who?" she asked.

He couldn't tell her. The vampires had proven that the human wasn't a threat, and he had panicked. It was bad enough that he was going to have to head inside, to face another pack's judgement all over again. He couldn't tell her he was weak as well.

"No one important."

She gave him a look, one that said she knew he wasn't telling the truth but also wasn't going to push the issue, and part of him softened.

"Then let's go," she said.

He rolled the window back up, shut off the car, and pulled his briefcase out with him as he left the vehicle. Len went slowly, stalling, trying everything to keep from going inside, into a pack's territory. Into something he could never have. But then he was out and following the woman inside the house through several rooms until they made it to an office.

An older man sat behind a desk. Gray dusted his dark brown hair, and small wrinkles appeared in the corners of his eyes. His skin was lighter than his heir's, but there was no denying that they were related.

"I'm Len." He held out his hand but yanked it back when he saw how much it was trembling. "I am associated with a conservation project that is happening in Ember, and Elizabeth thought it was best to meet."

The alpha stared off at his desk, as if distracted. Len's heartbeat picked up speed, and his breath caught. "Maybe there is a better time. I could come back later." *Or never.*

Phoenix stepped behind the desk and put her hand on her father's shoulder. He seemed almost to awaken at the touch. The alpha turned and looked directly at Len, as if taking in the very essence of him. Except Len wasn't pack, and that shouldn't have been possible.

"We were expecting you," the alpha said. "I see you've met my daughter."

"We … she … I know she is your heir."

"Introductions may seem trivial and like a waste of time," the alpha said, "but they are important for establishing a starting point. They can be used to put someone at ease, or even to establish dominance." He had turned toward his daughter, as if using this moment with a stranger to teach her. "As you have probably surmised, I am the alpha of the Ember pack. This is Phoenix, my daughter and my heir. You will meet with us both, but she will be responsible for any final decisions."

Len froze at the words. An alpha never ceded control. It went against their very nature. He tried not to let the astonishment show on his face. "I appreciate you both meeting with me today. I am uncertain how connected you have been to the conservation program. It may be best for me to tell you a bit about what we do."

He started talking, delivering the same introduction that he had given everyone. It was a lot of words trying to connect to the community, and some slight fearmongering against human encroachment—not too much, just enough that no one realized that he hadn't told them anything at all. He didn't have much of anything to say to them. Sure, he had gleaned some information over the years, but who ran the company and what they were trying to do was just as much a mystery to him.

The alpha wolf sat still, his eyes slightly unfocused, as if he were bored or had difficulty staying on track. Phoenix sat stoically next to him, but her leg bounced in the smallest of motions and her fingers tapped on the side of her thigh. He did the same thing when he needed to stay focused on something that was outside his interest.

"Why did you leave your pack?" Phoenix asked.

She had cut in while he was talking, the topic change so sudden that he froze where he was, unable to adjust enough even to answer.

"I know most alphas are all about posturing and mind games, and I find it all exhausting," Phoenix said. "However, I probably should not have been quite so blunt. We aren't especially interested in the conservation efforts that are currently happening. We are interested in you."

Len's heart rate spiked, pulsating through his entire body.

"You went through the naming ceremony?" Phoenix asked.

He nodded his head.

"You were given the name of Lennon."

She had said it as a statement, but he squeaked out a quiet, "Yes."

"Lennon means lover. That is what they had given you, but you chose another name. You go by Len, which means brave. Are you brave?"

"I try to be," he said.

"What made you give up your pack and your own identity?"

"My own identity?" Len said. "I am still myself."

"Are you? Our names are part of who we are, and you have abandoned yours to be something else. You are pretending to be who you think you need to be and have forgotten who you are."

Her voice came out sharp and strong like that of a full alpha, and Len felt the words pushing into himself. He didn't remember moving. One second he was sitting in the chair, and the next he was using it as an insufficient shield. He was folded in on himself, trying to clench his hands to keep them from shaking.

He was no longer a grown man. He was ten, hiding in a corner, trying to be as quiet as possible. The other boys had called him names and told on him. He felt the shame of who he was sink into him. The alpha was yelling at his mother, and he knew that he should come out and take his punishment. Instead, he stayed hidden, listening to the alpha explain what had happened. He had disgraced the pack.

Hands wrapped around him, and he leaned into the grasp.

"I'm sorry, Mommy. I'm so sorry. I will do better. It won't happen again. I'll be just like the other boys."

Except that the arms did not belong to his mother. He hadn't seen her since he had left. Len jumped up, putting his back against the bookshelf and staring down at the young alpha heir.

"I shouldn't have pushed you," she said. "I'm sorry."

He didn't know what to do with those words. Alphas didn't apologize, and he knew that she was the alpha of the pack, even if her father still wore the title. The older wolf sat at the desk, his eyes unfocused, unaware of everything that had just happened.

"He has good days and bad days," Phoenix said. "Today is a bad day."

"What is …" Len paused, uncertain how to continue.

"He has a form of dementia that is unique to our kind. There hasn't been a lot of research done on it. A lot of wolves would see it as a weakness, but my father is not weak. He is working with a specialist to hopefully help us to understand more of what is going on."

"That is why you are alpha."

"No."

Phoenix stepped forward as she spoke, and Len jerked back, still too raw. She realized what she had done and sunk back in her chair instead.

"My father is still alpha. I still have much to learn from him before I take over the pack. He makes judgements. I just have the final decision on the days that he is less clear."

Len couldn't help marveling at an alpha that would give away even a small bit of his power. His old alpha would have never let go. He would have run the pack into the ground until he was forced out of his position, but here there was a sharing and acknowledgement. It was such a unique idea that Len had a hard time believing it.

"I think we should go meet the pack," Phoenix said. She took her father's hand and guided him out of the room before Len could object.

Len trailed behind Phoenix and the alpha as she walked them around the main floor of their house. It was a typical pack house with a large kitchen and communal gathering areas. Down in the basement, there was a training center with gym equipment and a floor covered in sturdy mats. Just one wolf was working out this afternoon. He gave Len curious glances as he continued his workout. Len stayed close behind Phoenix and her father, trying to minimize the other wolf's attention.

They headed outside. The crisp fall air surrounded Len even as the sun still sat high in the sky. The leaves had started to turn, and as they walked through the neighborhood, the signs of fall were all around them.

"Does every pack member live in this area?" he asked.

"Yes," Phoenix said. "It is easier to stay together since we don't have to hide as much as other packs. Ember may be united, but it helps that each community has its own territory. We are able to build our houses with enough space so that we have real privacy, instead of just the illusion of it."

Phoenix walked in between a pair of houses, and Len followed like a lost, overwhelmed pup. Seeing the houses and the community had affected him in a way he hadn't expected. A deep sense of longing filled him. To have a place, one place, to call his own … to be able to spend the night in a bed that belonged just to him … it was more than he could think about. Being around a pack was beginning to affect him deeply. He was grateful for everything that the company had given him, but as much as he tried, they were not pack. They might have kept him grounded for the last decade, but they didn't understand the need to transform and run into the night. They didn't know what it was like to lie down in fur, huddled around those you called family.

Behind the houses was an open field that backed up into mountainous forest terrain.

"There are over two hundred acres that are pack-owned," Phoenix said. "This isn't counting the residential space. This is just the wilderness we have set aside for roaming. The humans believe that a wolf pack was reintroduced in the area, so they know to expect wolves, and the bordering area is surrounded by other magical communities, so we rarely have any problems."

Len couldn't help the longing entering his heart as he looked at the wilderness. He smelled pine, water, and even a deer path. It reminded him so much of his home back in Montana.

"How long has it been since you shifted?" Phoenix asked.

"I move around too fast. It has been a while since there has been a safe enough space."

"We could go for a run."

Len looked down at his khaki pants, business shirt, and tie. His wolf seemed like it belonged to another person, locked away for so long he wasn't even sure that he could call it out.

"I almost wasn't named heir," Phoenix said. "I was diagnosed as autistic at a very young age. My father had concerns about whether I would be able to handle the pack. Eventually, I was named heir, and my cousin, the second son, was kicked out of the pack. It could have been me, and I thought about what I would do if it happened. It was so hard to even consider. I can't imagine how difficult it must have been for you to be forced to leave."

Phoenix stood stoic, her hand steadying her father's arm as she looked out at the wilderness, giving Len time to process her words.

"Our pack was sent to school with the human children. There were six of us in total in the elementary school in the nearest town," Len said. "They thought we were some kind of cult, or at least an eccentric community. I guess they were not too far off. At the teacher's insistence, my mother took me to a psychologist, where I was diagnosed with ADHD. It was such a foreign concept to our alpha. He kept insisting that I just needed to spend more time with the men, that I needed to play outside more. Somehow, that was supposed to solve all my problems."

"It is hard when those around you don't understand," Phoenix said.

The alpha started turning, making his way back to the main house, and Phoenix let go of his arm before walking behind him. Len kept pace beside her.

"Do you miss your pack?"

Len thought about the question before answering. "I miss my mother. I know that leaving was best for her, allowing her to stay with her family, but I do wish that I could talk to her again."

"Would you bring her with you when you find a new pack?"

The question cut deep, and a longing opened up in his soul—one he closed quickly.

"The company is my pack."

Phoenix glanced at him, but didn't call him on his lie. They both knew that a pack required other wolves, or at least a community that wasn't separated and controlled by management. But they were all he had, and were all he would have, so he tried not to dwell on it.

They walked back through the residence in silence until they entered the main house. The alpha was already inside and was sitting down on a couch in a common area. Sitting right next to him was Ancel.

Ancel was smiling, talking to the older wolf. It was the type of smile that lit up a room, and Len felt his heart start to beat so fast he was afraid it would burst through his chest. Then Ancel reached up and fixed his hair, pushing the short bangs out of his eyes. Len thought he might melt straight through the floor.

He wanted to run. It was past time that he leave this town, but there was still work to be done. Instead, he closed his eyes, breathing deeply until he was able to bring his heart rate back under control.

They had left the alpha and Ancel back in the community room. Len felt safer in the office, better able to pull back on his business persona. That is what he was good at, what he had perfected over the last decade.

"Thank you for giving me a tour of your territory. It helped me better understand Ember and how this project will interact with all the communities in this town. I have visited most of North America, and I can say that this town is unique in the way you have all managed to come together. Do you have any questions about what we are doing with the conservation project?"

Phoenix didn't answer. She just sat behind the large desk, studying him curiously.

"Do you mind if I call you Lennon?" she finally asked.

He desperately wanted to be Lennon, to be permitted to become the person he was promised on his naming day. But that part of him was in the past, no longer allowed. It had cost him his pack ... and his family. Now he just used it because it sounded more professional, a jagged cut to his heart to remind him he could never be himself.

"Please use the name that you are most comfortable with," he said.

"Lennon, I still don't understand what happened with your old pack. I understand that you felt you had to leave, and are doing the best you can in the current circumstances. I am very direct and would appreciate you telling me everything that has happened, but I have been cautioned that not everyone is as direct as I am. That being said, I feel confident that you will do well here. Both Elizabeth and Birk have spoken highly of you, and I give their opinions a lot of weight. I am prepared to offer you a place in our pack."

Len froze. His mind sputtered to catch up to what the alpha heir had said. "A place ... in your pack?"

"Yes."

His mind spun with the possibilities. He could have a house, territory, a place to run.

The alpha shuffled into the room, and settled into the chair next to Phoenix.

"I should be here," he said. "I should be here when a membership offer is extended."

Phoenix gave him a nod.

Len smelled the other wolf before he heard him standing perched in the doorway.

"You should join us," Phoenix said.

It took Len a moment to realize that she had been talking to Ancel.

"I don't think I should," he said.

"Sit down, son," the alpha said.

With that, Ancel sat in the seat next to Len, the one next to the door. Suddenly, Len couldn't breathe. He needed to get away, but there was nowhere to go.

"Our pack was one of the founding communities of Ember," the alpha said. "We are proud, but we have learned much by living near the other creatures. We understand that you would still need to travel for work. We discussed that before … when I was thinking more clearly. You would be a good addition to our pack."

"How long have you known you were going to offer me a place in your pack? When did you talk to the vampires? Did the company put you up to this?"

Rage started to flare, taking over his anxiety. Had he just been a pawn in a game that everyone except him had been playing? Was he so all over the place that it required other people to decide his future for him?

"It's okay, Lennon." Ancel laid his hand over Len's.

Len watched Ancel's fingers gently squeeze his own as his blood flowed all through his body, and he knew that he couldn't stay here in this pack … with Ancel … They would know how he felt about the other wolf.

He shot up out of his seat, grabbing his briefcase from under the chair where he had left it earlier. "Thank you for the offer. I appreciate it, but I do not think that I should join your pack."

"Why?" Phoenix asked.

A million answers fluttered through Len's mind,

none of them reaching his mouth. He didn't need to speak; Ancel spoke for him.

"He can't stay because I am attracted to him."

Len stared down at the other wolf. He must have said it wrong. Even now, he must be trying to save Len the embarrassment of his attraction.

"You're attracted to him. He is attracted to you. Who cares? As long as anything you do is mutually consensual, you are allowed to have relations among pack members."

Len looked at Phoenix, trying to understand what she was saying. Then he studied Ancel again, letting himself pay attention to his senses. He could smell the slight scent of arousal, as well as shame. He had done that to the other man. "You're gay? You know that he is gay?" It wasn't the most brilliant thing he could have said, but the idea still mystified him.

"Oh," Phoenix said. "That is why you were sent away from your pack."

He let the briefcase fall out of his hands onto the empty chair. It had become too heavy to carry.

The alpha sat watching the conversation, his gaze focused, unlike earlier in the day. "I had a hard time understanding at first," he said. "I saw the way the other pups treated Ancel, and I thought that it was important for him to be a man. Then he became my daughter's friend, and I saw the way that he protected her—they protected each other—and I made sure everyone knew that he was pack, exactly how he was. That doesn't mean he had it easy, and part of that was my fault. I saw so much of myself in my second son that

I didn't notice how he was treating the other wolves. Even now, I still have room to learn and grow. I can promise you that you will be accepted and safe here. You would be brought into the pack knowing who you are. You wouldn't have to hide."

Len's eyes watered. The tears threatened to spill over, but one did not cry in front of the alpha.

"I didn't know you were attracted to me," Len said instead to Ancel. "I learned long ago not to show that part of myself around other wolves. I haven't been doing very well at it since I have been here."

"Great, so now that this is cleared up, you can join," Phoenix said.

"I …" Len wasn't sure how to put his thoughts into words. They were busy bouncing around in his skull, unable to settle. It was all too much, too fast. Everything he could have ever dreamed of and every way that he would mess it up played out simultaneously before his eyes. "I need some time."

He saw a flash of hurt shine in Ancel's eyes and confusion on Phoenix's face.

"It's not 'no', it's just …"

"It's too much good too fast. You don't trust it," Ancel said.

"Yeah."

Ancel reached out tentatively, wrapping his fingers between Len's before giving them a slight squeeze and letting go.

"I understand," Phoenix said. "At least I think I do."

"Come back in the morning," the alpha said.

They all knew that in the morning, he would say

yes, but for now, he needed to escape the room. There was not enough space to breathe. He picked up his suitcase again, clutching it in front of his body like a shield, and slipped behind Ancel's chair. Then he was out of the office, then out of the house, and finally back in his rental car. Only then could he feel the air entering his lungs.

The sun had just set behind the mountain as Len pulled into the hotel parking lot. He barely remembered the drive from the pack house. His mind was too busy thinking through all the possible ways that tomorrow would go wrong. They would rescind the offer of the pack for sure once they realized how scattered he was and how much of a mess he was. Maybe they had just made the offer in the first place out of pity. They'd felt bad for him, and while that might not be the worst thing, it would still leave him with a pack. However, he wasn't sure he could handle being pitied for the rest of his life.

Then there was Ancel. Just thinking about his smile made Len … Lennon's stomach flutter. It had to all be a cruel trick to be taken from him as soon as he started to believe that this could be his life.

Lennon opened up the door to his car, forgetting his suitcase on the seat, as he walked toward the hotel.

He didn't recognize the scent of the human until it

was too late. A sharp pain hit his lower back—a strong shock shooting through his body. If he hadn't been a werewolf, it would have knocked him down. Instead, he turned to see the startled human was holding a camera in one hand and a black, gun-shaped object in his other hand. A wire was hanging out of the end of it that led to Lennon's back.

Before Lennon's mind had fully processed what was happening, the human dropped the taser on the ground. He reached into his back pocket and pulled out an even larger taser and fired it directly at Lennon. His body seized with the intense shock of electricity, and he fell to the ground, convulsing.

"As you can see, the specimen was not impacted by the taser designed for humans. It needed the one built for large prey, such as bears. This inconclusively proves that we are dealing with something that is not human. As I have shown in my other videos, this creature is supernatural. We will need to secure him to determine exactly what kind of creature he is. Although I am confident that with time it will be found that he is a Sasquatch that has adapted over time to pass among us humans.

"I will need to put you all down so that I can secure this monster for my safety."

Lennon felt plastic bands being wrapped around his wrists and ankles. He tried to resist. A human shouldn't be able to take down a werewolf. But his limbs refused to cooperate, and it took everything he had to remain alert. He tried to struggle against the plastic bands, but his muscles refused to do more than jerk around. Then the human's hands came rushing toward his face, holding the large taser. It crashed against his skull, and then darkness overcame him.

When he woke up, it was dark. He could feel rumbling underneath him, and it wasn't too hard to determine that he had been stuffed into a trunk. His legs were bent to get his tall frame in, and he was having difficulty feeling them.

A fine mesh of wire was wrapped all around him.

"Ignorant human," he muttered. Silver didn't do anything to werewolves; that was just another myth perpetuated by popular media. However, the wires were digging into his skin, causing what felt like small cuts anywhere his clothing wasn't thick enough to protect him.

He struggled to get his hands, bound behind him, out of the wire, but it was tied too tightly, and it just caused his hands to become slick with blood. As his eyes adjusted to the darkness, he started to take in his surroundings. Right above him was a pull tab to open the trunk. He tried to lift his body enough that he could snatch it with his teeth, but there wasn't room for him to maneuver.

His hands moved around searching for anything behind him and found a long metal object. It felt like it could be a tripod for a camera that the naive human had left in the car. It wasn't very sturdy, and there wasn't much that he could do with it, as his hands were constrained behind his back, but he gripped it tightly anyway.

Lennon tried to think of something that he could do. He wasn't going to go down as the werewolf that had been taken by a human. He wasn't going to give up when there was a pack waiting to take him in, and maybe there was a wolf who wanted to explore the possibility of … something. Even now, his mind wouldn't let him grasp on to that possibility. It was too much to hope for.

Instead, he started pushing out with his legs, attempting to hit the back of the trunk. As he moved them, the blood started flowing back in, and the sensation of pins and needles collided with the metal cutting into his slacks, but at least he could feel them again. He was able to push out with more and more force. The angle wasn't great, but he was a werewolf and had enough power to cause the back of the trunk to start vibrating.

Lennon remembered a true crime story he had watched one late night at a hotel. A woman was trapped in the trunk and had kicked out the taillight, causing the police to pull the vehicle over. He wasn't sure it would work … but at least it was something.

The car began to slow, and Lennon braced himself. The tripod was in his hands, and his legs were ready to push once more. He was not going to be taken unaware as easily again.

"This is truly phenomenal," the human's voice filtered through the trunk. "The creature appears to have withstood the silver mesh enough to become aggressive. I will carefully open the trunk to taser it once again to teach it to stop its aggressive behavior. It is not unlike Pavlov and his dog."

Lennon was ready as the trunk began to open. He didn't wait, but kicked his legs toward the human, causing the camera to slip out of the man's hands. He then kicked out again. His legs stretched out of the trunk enough that he was able to tip his body out. Except that he didn't land on his feet. With everything wrapped up, he lost his balance, falling on the ground and rolling right off the edge of the cliff that the car was parked next to. He fell, splashing into the river that ran through Ember.

His hands couldn't break free from the mesh, and his legs were not able to move enough to navigate the current. He sunk lower as the rapids pushed him forward. His body hit rocks as the current swept him away. He struggled to get control, but his head stayed under the water, and although he held his breath as long as he could, his lungs finally demanded release.

They were met with a torrent of water.

Hands wrapped around him, lifting his head above the surface. Then, unprompted, water was expelled from his lungs as if by magic. He gulped in air, relishing it even as it hit his raw throat. Then he was moving, being dragged along the top of the river, with very little concern for access to oxygen or the impact of the water as it crashed against his skin. He tried to time his breaths for when he would be able to take in air, but wasn't always successful.

By the time he was thrown onto a small island in the middle of the river, he was gasping for breath. His entire body hurt from the electrical charge and from the water seeping into the cuts all over his skin. The ground seemed to be moving beneath him, and part of him still felt like he was drowning.

He took his time before he carefully rolled over enough to take in the merperson who had dragged him to safety. They were waiting a few feet out in the water, staring at him. Lennon knew that he had not been saved. If there were merpeople in the river, as there obviously were, then they claimed this as their territory and would fiercely defend it.

The merperson had a slight blue tinge to their light skin. Their jaw was square-cut with deep gills that were often found on males, but they wore their hair free with their chest covered like most female merpeople.

"What do I call you?" Lennon asked.

The merperson stared at him, their face hard. But they weren't showing any teeth, something Lennon knew from personal experience was a good thing.

"I am Janavi, daughter of Mairead. Why was a wolf in our river? You do not belong to Phoenix, daughter of the Ember Pack." The words came out with a lyrical hiss, an accent that all merpeople had when trying to speak English, a sharp contrast to their native tongue that was more melody than words.

"I ..." Lennon wasn't sure how to explain. He had only talked to one other merpeople pod when he had been sent to Mississippi. It hadn't gone well, and he had been thankful to have walked away alive. But these merpeople were used to interacting with other magical creatures. Maybe they would understand. "I was sent here to meet with one of the nymphs ..."

Before he could continue, Janavi charged forward, her mouth open in a hiss, exposing her fangs. Her tail raised and crashed suddenly, causing a torrent of water to cover his already soaked form.

"We do not like friends of the child killers," she hissed.

Lennon tried to move back, but the metal wiring

was not giving way. If anything, it was tighter than when he'd first woken up.

"I don't know what you mean," he said. "I met with Birk—the one who had been cast out. We are working on a project together. I met with Phoenix, and she extended me an invitation to join her pack. I'm not pack yet, but I will be."

He knew his voice was desperate and pleading. The merpeople liked confidence and strength, but the terror flowing from his body was more than he could handle. He had heard that merpeople would occasionally eat trespassers alive. The protein helped them to survive the colder season, and winter was fast approaching.

But she had stopped and was looking at him quizzically. This close, he could see her deep brown eyes and the scar on her shoulder where her birthname had been cut off and replaced with her true name.

"That does not explain why you are in our water."

"There was a human. He caught me and wrapped me up. I tried to escape, but tripped and fell over the side of the cliff into the river. If you hadn't found me, I would have drowned."

She opened her mouth wide, tilting her chin up, and let out a laugh that sounded like breaking glass. It continued for more than a minute, and Lennon knew that he had lost her respect. She would no longer let him go. It was up to him to escape.

"What a weak wolf to get caught by a human," she said once the laughing had stopped. "You are here alone. No pack, no friends, no pod. No one will miss you. They will not even know where you have gone."

He started shaking at the words, because she was right. When he didn't show up in the morning to join the pack, they would assume that he was too scared. Everyone would think that he had run off, leaving everything behind. Even his mother wouldn't notice. Her payments would continue until his bank account dried up, but that would be many years in the future. At most, a few of his bones would wash onto the shore with teeth marks gnawed into them.

His vision blanked out, and he started to flail, trying to break free from the metal. All it did was cause it to dig into his skin even further, but he couldn't stop. He needed to get out before the merperson hauled him into the water and brought him back to her pod.

She laughed again, the sound breaking into his panic. Then she began to taunt him, gliding around the island, flicking her tail to send water flying, and hissing when she came into view. Her eyes opened wide, allowing them to double in size, and the gills on the side of her neck flared open for even more intimidation.

"I'm going to bring you home for supper," she said. "Mommy will be so proud. All the children will laugh with glee at the dinner I brought home."

For a brief moment, he saw his mother in his mind. She was smiling at him, wiping away his tears. "It's okay to be afraid, love. Fear lets us know that we are alive. What you have to learn is when to acknowledge the fear and when to push back against it and rise up."

"I need to rise up, Mommy," he said.

Lennon attempted to block out Janavi's voice, but the more she kept taunting, the more she fell back into the merpeople's native tongue. It was no longer words as much as musical notes, dark tones that called for his death.

He focused on the wiring, trying to determine if he could find where it ended and somehow unwrap himself from it. The futility of that became apparent when he realized that even if he somehow managed to get the wire off, there were still plastic strips around his arms and legs. The ones on his legs looked thick, with a separate enclosure for each of his ankles. The human had come prepared.

It only left one option, and if Lennon had been true to his werewolf, instead of trying to deny his existence, he would have done it long ago. It was time to call his wolf. He closed his eyes, doing all he could to tune out the noise and the dampness. He tried to ignore that the ritual taking place out in the river was sure to end soon, and he would be dragged under the water where his wolf would drown as surely as his human body. Instead, he focused on the place where the other half of himself lived.

When he was young, the space between his halves had been almost nonexistent. He would come home from school and change into his wolf as soon as his backpack hit the ground. Changing was not hard. It was just calling a different self into existence, a self that seemed to live in its own pocket universe, just waiting to get out.

Except it had been years since he had shifted. There were always excuses, but the truth was it was too hard to be in his wolf without a pack around him. So he had locked that part of himself away and tried not to think too hard about it. And now, when he needed it to emerge, it was nowhere to be found. The connection was missing. It wasn't even like hitting a brick wall or a disconnected conduit—it was just gone.

Tears started streaming down his face. It was a weakness that the merpeople would not approve of, but Lennon no longer cared. The memory of the last time he had called on his wolf crashed into him. It had been two years after he had left the pack. The organization had sent him back to Montana to meet with a nymph family. After, he had shifted, running through the hills, so much like his youth. The pain had hit him all at once, the loneliness that the organization would never be able to feel. So he had done the only thing he'd known how to do—he'd stopped feeling. Lennon had let the wolf go, slipping on his human form and ignoring the pain and isolation, pretended that the organization was enough for him to survive, because it was all that he had.

Now he was going to die, torn apart by merpeople for their dinner, as the facade he had built started to fall apart, as if it was made of little more than paper and tape that he had held together over the years by sheer force of will. If he was going to die, then he would do so as himself, no matter how it seemed to others. He was so tired of trying so hard to be something else for the organization. He might have difficulty remembering some things or losing track of time. Maybe he was a bit paranoid, but he also had been right. There was a human out to get him, and he had turned out to be a danger. Too bad no one would ever know.

Lennon let go of the pressure. He let go of the false belief and the masking. In the end, he wanted to die as himself. His body relaxed into the inevitable, and there he saw his wolf. His tears shifted from sadness to joy, and he reached out to the part that he had cut off for too long and found himself covered in fur.

His human form had shifted, taking his clothes and the entrapment with it. He now had free use of his limbs. He stretched out his legs that had not been used in so long, and felt relief that they were whole. With the pain of his human body gone, he could focus once again.

The merperson had stopped and was looking at him. Lennon went up to the water's edge and let out a hiss of his own that turned into a low growl. Then he lifted his face into the air and howled.

They began a simple dance, with Lennon lunging at the merperson and her gliding back out of reach of his jaws. Then she would hiss, charging forward, splashing her tail in the water and sending a wave his way. Soon, he was as drenched in his wolf form as he had been in his human form.

He tried circling the small island. It was less than ten feet wide, and as soon as he made it to the other side, the merperson joined him. He was trapped. Most likely, he would still end up dinner, but at least he would go down fighting.

Lennon charged into the water, catching the merperson off guard and drawing teeth marks across her arm. He lunged back fast enough to escape her talon-shaped fingers. There she was beached in the shallow part of the water, and he tried to take advantage of the situation. He dug his jaw into her arm and attempted to drag her to the beach, stranding her enough that he could get away, but her jaw clamped through his fur, her razor-sharp teeth piercing his flesh, and he let go. A trail of blood followed him as he retreated from the water.

Janavi used her uninjured arm to push herself back out to the river, the whole time baring her fangs in warning. Lennon held back. He was stronger in his wolf, but he had never been a fighter. His strength was in doing the unexpected.

With the merperson injured, he hoped to be able to outrun her, even with his side screaming out with his own pain. He feinted, trying to throw the merperson off enough that he could create an opening to swim out. He moved as rapidly as he could on three legs, circling his little island as the merperson kept up with ease, her injury no longer a hindrance in the water.

He stopped, trying to determine a better strategy, when he realized she was gone. His eyes dashed around the ground, afraid that she had somehow made it near him, but then he caught her off in the distance, swimming away, her long tail propelling her forward faster than he could imagine. She didn't even look back.

Without wasting any more time, he jumped into the river. He had no idea where he was, so he guessed what bank to swim to and started paddling as fast as he could. The current was swift, and his legs were not strong enough to make much progress. Soon, his muzzle was dipping under the water, but he was determined not to give up. He kept paddling, taking breaths when he broke the surface. As he became tired, a part of him wanted to give in to the river, letting it take him, but he ignored that part of himself. He wasn't going to allow himself to drown now, not this close to getting what he wanted. There was a new pack out there willing to take him in, and someone who could maybe one day love him for exactly who he was.

As the river washed over him, his legs no longer able to help him break the surface, he pictured Ancel's face one last time. Maybe they would find him, and at least now they hopefully would know what had happened to him.

rms wrapped around him, pulling his head above the water. They held him up even as the river threatened to send him under again. Even as the water coated his nostrils, he could smell Ancel next to him, the scent of forest and spicy aftershave. He let out a small yip in appreciation for the rescue, but it caused more of the river to flow into his mouth.

"Just hold on," Ancel said. "You almost made it to the edge. There isn't that much farther left to go."

The words lifted Lennon. He might have almost drowned, needing his knight to come and save him, but he had tried. He had almost succeeded.

One of Ancel's arms gripped tightly around his midsection as the werewolf used his free arm and feet to propel them forward. Lennon tried to assist, using a reserve he didn't know he had to paddle with his three uninjured legs.

It wasn't long before the shore came into view. Then Ancel was standing up, bringing Lennon out of the river and completely into his arms. A cascade of water fell off Lennon's red fur as he was lifted. When they were on land, Ancel still didn't let him go. He held Lennon's bulk close to his chest. Lennon placed his muzzle on his shoulder and, careful to make sure his claws were out of the way, snuggled into his bare chest. Then, before he could think better of it, he flicked his tongue over Ancel's cheek.

Ancel laughed; then he squeezed Lennon tight and buried his head into his fur. "I almost lost you before I even got to know you."

He was grateful that he was a wolf and didn't have to reply.

Ancel started walking along the riverbank. Lennon could have walked, now that he had air in his lungs and the current was no longer restricting his movements. But Ancel did not seem inclined to put him down, and Lennon felt a sense of peace lying in his arms.

"You found him," Phoenix said.

Lennon lifted his head enough to see the heir standing near the bank. Her hand was clasped around the human's neck. Lennon let out a low growl upon seeing him. However, there was very little risk that the human would be able to break away from her.

"I found him near the bottom of the river," Ancel said. "The brave mutt decided to swim for it."

No one had ever called him brave before, and the word settled into him, warming him.

"That is only because I let him live."

Lennon startled at the voice, jumping clear out of Ancel's arms and landing on his paws. He bent low in the dirt and started growling toward the river, where the merperson bobbed in the water.

"Enough," Phoenix said.

He stopped growling instantly, but kept his teeth bared.

"This wolf is mine," Phoenix said. "Make sure your siblings know that he has been accepted into the Ember Pack and is not to come to harm."

"You cannot hold us accountable for what has happened. The wolf was saved and barely harmed in my care. There was but one bite taken out of his flesh. Besides, there was nothing to suggest he belonged to you."

"He is a werewolf," Ancel said. He stopped talking at the glance from Phoenix.

"If we were to come across one of your kind that we had not previously met, wouldn't you want us to consult with you first? We could confirm they were kin, or if they did not come from your pod, we would let you handle the intruder. Any wolf in Ember belongs under my domain. I should have been notified immediately that he was in your care. I shouldn't have found out he fell in the river from the human."

The merperson opened her mouth, showing the rows of her pointed teeth before speaking. "In the interest of ... *peace* ... we will do what you ask. We expect the same in return."

"Thank you. I can see you caused my wolf no permanent harm—"

Lennon couldn't stop the low growl that emitted from his abdomen.

"Little physical harm, at least. We are glad that all misunderstandings have been cleared up, and continue to live according to the treaty. If you are ever in need of assistance, we stand ready to help."

Lennon felt Phoenix's gaze on him, assessing him to make sure that he was not, in fact, severely hurt. He felt … fine, despite his injury. His wolf was tired and wet. He wouldn't mind curling up for a nap, and it would be a heck of a show when he returned to human form covered in a mesh of wire, but not only had he survived, he had found his wolf once again.

"What about the human?" Janavi asked.

They all turned their attention back to the merperson, who was still in the river, despite Phoenix's obvious dismissal. She was looking the human up and down and moving her blue tongue over her lips like she was thinking about how tasty he would be marinated in river water.

Lennon considered himself a pacifist. He wouldn't even hurt a spider if it were trapped in one of his hotel rooms. Instead, they shared the space until it was Lennon who eventually left, but some part of himself was not upset by the idea of giving the human to the merpeople, and he wasn't sure how he felt about that.

"The human will be handed to the council for them to decide what will happen to him," Phoenix said.

The merperson laughed, as sharp as diamonds drilling into one's skull, and Lennon found himself backing up until he felt the reassuring presence of Ancel's legs behind him. Ancel dropped to his knees and wrapped an arm around Lennon, and for once, he couldn't tell who was comforting whom.

"How will you contain him?" Janavi said. "Do you have a cell to throw him into? Maybe you will take him to the vampires and hope they do not suck him dry. No, give him to me, and I will trap him under the water, unable to escape until the council calls for him."

"How would he fare any better with you than the vampires? He must be judged by the council, not served for your dinner."

A faint scent of urine filtered on the breeze, and Lennon looked over to see the human still firmly in Phoenix's grasp despite his struggles otherwise. His pants were now soiled from fear.

Lennon knew what it was like to feel that kind of fear, and it didn't give him any pleasure to see the human in the same state. However, it did seem like a sense of justice.

"I will not eat him. His bones will not feel a single graze of my teeth. His skin will not be broken by me or my siblings, and his lungs will stay filled with air. Do you doubt my word?"

Phoenix paused, studying the merperson as if she were a puzzle that made no sense. "Why?" she finally asked.

"I am bored. Guarding the human will be fun. But your kind is not the only one that will be impacted if his knowledge gets out. At least those on land can find other fields and forests. Where will the river dwellers go? Our cousins will not take us in, because we are not so kind to each other. If we are discovered, my pod will perish. I will hold him because it must be done, and I will not harm him, because the treaty demands it. However, I will enjoy my time while he is with me."

Lennon watched the alpha heir glance at Ancel for his opinion. He had never seen a dominant look to a submissive for consultation. Ancel shrugged and said, "It may be the best option."

To Lennon's amazement, that was all it took before Phoenix was hauling the human into the river and handing him over to the merperson. The human screamed as he exchanged hands, but the sound was soon gone as he was plunged under the water. There were only a few bubbles where he had gone down. By the time Phoenix made it back out, there was no sign of either of them.

"I hope I did the right thing," Phoenix said.

"That is all we can ever hope for," Ancel said. "Shall we take our new pack member home?"

And it was then that Lennon realized that these two were friends—a dominant and a submissive—and he felt a deep sense of hope for his own future.

The doors to the house were propped open. So many people were entering and exiting, they would have been in constant motion otherwise. With just over a hundred adult pack members, it wasn't that it was the largest pack. There had been nearly five hundred in Lennon's old pack, all spread across Montana's open range. But the pack hadn't gathered all that often when he had been young. He'd only known the other pups because they had been forced into the same school.

They had never held an event like this. Adding new pack members had been a private affair between the alpha and the individual, and that had been that.

There had been a ceremony with a few key members of the Ember Pack earlier, to officially add Lennon to pack ranks, a formality held together by tradition. Now it was a party.

The last few hours had been a whirlwind of new names and faces, all welcoming him. If anyone had any concerns about the situation, they hadn't let it show. There had been hugs that had stopped after the first few times he'd tensed up, followed by hand clasps and fist bumps.

Now Lennon sat in the corner of the game room in a comfortable chair that didn't catch all the light. He was watching a group of pups playing at a pool table that was only slightly shorter than their shoulders.

"This is where Phoenix goes when she still needs to be a part of the pack, but is too overwhelmed," Ancel said.

Lennon had seen him slowly approaching, giving him ample time to wave him away or give some other indication of wanting to be alone.

"It has been a long time since I have been around so many other wolves."

"Every wolf here has chosen to stay once Phoenix was made heir," Ancel said. "She was very open about her expectations within the pack. No one should give you trouble, but if anyone does, let her know, and it will be dealt with."

"Were there people who had left?"

"A few." Ancel settled into the second chair. It seemed to fit him, like it was his usual place next to Phoenix. "A few more left when the announcement about the alpha was given. We picked up several new pack members as well. Some other neurodivergent wolves have moved in, and a couple of families who have autistic pups."

"Do they all get parties this elaborate?"

"I suppose now is not a good time to tell you that

this happens about once a week. Phoenix is very big on the pack getting together."

Lennon's eyes must have given away his discomfort, because Ancel gave a laugh.

"You don't have to come," he said. "And if you do, this space is always open to you. There are a few more spots that are calmer around the house that I can show you."

"You and Phoenix seem very close."

"She is my best friend."

"It's unusual for a dominant and a submissive to be friends, especially one who is heir."

"Ember is full of the unusual. Our pack is no exception. She protected me when no one else did. She will protect you as well. Hopefully, in time, you will feel safe here."

"It … I … I don't feel unsafe here."

Ancel smiled at him and reached over, slowly, and grasped his fingers. Lennon felt his cheeks flush and his heart thump.

"I'm due to help out in the kitchen. I just wanted to make sure you were doing okay."

"I should come help."

"There will be plenty of time for that. Tonight is your night to sit back and be pampered. I'll bring you some more food when it is ready."

Lennon was going to protest. There had already been an abundance of snacking. Over the years, he had grown used to limiting his portions to appear more human, and he hadn't seen this much food in years, but before he could get any of it out, Ancel had returned to the kitchen.

He sat watching the pups play until they abandoned their game to get into some sort of mischief. The room was surprisingly quiet for how crowded the house was. What he was not expecting was for the heir to walk in carrying two plates of food.

Lennon jumped forward to take the plates from her, before she laughed and told him to sit down. She handed him a plate before sitting down.

"I heard this was your chair. I can move," Lennon said.

"There are no assigned seats in this pack house. I'm not sure if you have heard, but I'm not a big fan of dominance games. I know there is a time and place where they have to happen. I also understand that they will continue happening below me with the rest of the pack. I'm not naive, but I also don't see a reason that we have to keep acting the same way just because it is how it has been done for hundreds of years."

"It's innate," Lennon said.

"Is it? I'm not saying to abolish packs or eliminate alphas. There still needs to be structure and order, but I also don't believe my place in our pack makes me any smarter or better than anyone else. I don't want to lead out of fear."

Phoenix picked up the fork that had been balanced on her plate and took a bite. Lennon studied his own plate. There was a nice helping of beef sirloin and a variety of vegetables. The aroma hit him, and he realized how hungry he had become.

"I understand the need to fit into your environment," Phoenix said. "You have been away from a pack for a long while, and it will take you time to adjust. If you need more grace, then I'll give it. Let me know. However, what isn't up for debate is your health. You are a wolf, and you will begin taking care of yourself as a wolf. Which means eating enough."

Lennon picked up his fork, chastised. He took a bite and savored the taste as he chewed. They didn't talk to each other as they ate, just enjoyed eating in the quiet. Only the echoes of the pack surrounded them, and it occurred to Lennon that Phoenix had arranged this time deliberately.

Phoenix waited to speak until Lennon had reluctantly finished the last of his plate. "There is a group of therapists in town that work with the magical community. One of them belongs to the pack. I am not sure who you would be most comfortable working with, but I ask that you give it a try."

Lennon hadn't been expecting that.

"I understand you travel quite a bit for your job," she said. "I am hopeful the organization will let you settle into the pack some. You have been away a long time."

"I haven't heard from them," Lennon said. "My contact hasn't gotten back to me. I'm starting to get concerned."

Phoenix shifted in her seat. "I see. I'm not well-versed in what exactly your employment does, or their goal in Ember. I have only recently started sitting in the council meetings in my father's stead. If there is anything of concern that we need to be aware of regarding the pack or you, then please let me know. Otherwise, I just hope that all is well and they are giving you space to settle into your new family."

"I will," Lennon said. Suddenly, he was overcome with having two separate divisions to give his loyalty to. The organization had been his pack for so long, but now … now he had a home … a family.

"Your mother," Phoenix said. "Do you think that she would like to join the pack?"

Lennon started. Having Phoenix offer caused his eyes to start to water. "I don't think so. I left because she needed her pack, and I don't think that has changed. But … maybe … it would be okay for her to visit?"

"I'll start communication with her pack. If there are any complications, I will keep you informed. I have one last thing I want to say before I let you settle in. Ancel is a good friend of mine. I have known him for many years. He is also incredibly patient. He knows you need time to settle in, and he will be a good friend to you. If, at some point in the future, you decide to be more than friends, I know he will make a good mate. I would just like you to remember that you have been through a lot. It is not only okay, but it is essential, that you give yourself time before you rush into anything. That is not only fair for you, but for Ancel as well."

Lennon wasn't sure what to say to that, but Phoenix had stood up, taken both their plates, and was at the door before he had time to process all the words.

"Oh," she said. "The pixies brought over your items earlier. They are in the guest bedroom on the second floor. Ancel can show you when you are ready for a break. They also mentioned that they would like to grab a beer the next time you go hang out at Rocko's."

Well, that would be an experience.

It wasn't long before the pack started filtering in through the room again, and Lennon sat back, listening to his new family.

It was a few hours before he made it up to his room. Ancel had given him a brief hug before leaving him to look at his temporary space. It wasn't his bed, not exactly, but it was more permanent than a hotel room. The room smelled like pack—forests and fresh mountain air.

He had unpacked his suitcase into the dresser and plugged in his phone, when it started to ring. Danni's image popped up on the screen.

"Hello," he said. "Is everything okay? I have been trying to get a hold of you."

"No," Danni replied. "There is a problem with the project. I need you to stay in Ember. I am at the airport and will be there by tomorrow morning."

"So cold. Look at you shivering. You could make a fire." Janavi laughed at her joke. The cave was too wet for fire. It had no place for smoke to go. It only had oxygen because she had gifted it with her own.

The human didn't look pleased. The river still clung to his clothes, pooling underneath where he sat. His lips had a tinge of blue, almost like a proper merperson, and his body was shivering. Janavi bobbed in the center of the cavern in the water that flowed from the river. There was no way out except the river below. Its current ran underground for half a mile before the rock gave way to the river surface. It was insurmountable without the aid of her kind, but the human did not seem to understand his position.

"I have information back at the hotel. I can give you everything you need to destroy those monsters," he said.

Janavi laughed again, the sound echoing through the small cavern. "I am the monster, little human." She opened her mouth wide, showing the points of her teeth before snapping her jaw closed. A thrill shot through her when he flinched back against the cave wall.

His shadow bobbed along beside him. The only illumination came from a waterproof flashlight given by the nymphs. It was one of the many gifts they had presented in exchange for helping to rescue their children. Now it inched closer to the pool of water every time the small tide hit it. The man eyed it wearily, then glanced back at Janavi. It was only a few feet from where he sat, but he seemed frozen in fear.

"See, you shake now that you are no longer in charge. There is no wire here to wrap me in, only water —endless water. I have not told my siblings that you are here. If anything happens to me, you will die all alone … cold and hungry." She cackled, once again relishing as he shook, partially in terror and mostly with cold. Humans were so fragile.

"Let me out and I will help you," he said. His voice was quiet and lacked conviction.

"We can play a game, human. You can jump into this pool and swim to the surface. If you make it, then you get freedom."

"And if I don't?"

"Then I get to watch you die."

He inched closer to the edge of the pool, peering into its dark depths. His face scrunched up in concentration, and for a moment, she wondered if she would get some good entertainment for the night. It would be easy to tell the council that he had drowned—as long as she gave his body back without teeth marks.

But he scooted back against the wall and closed his eyes. Her fun for the night was over. But there was one last thing she could do. Janavi propelled her body up high enough in the water so he could see the start of her fin and grabbed the wobbling flashlight before plunging into the depths.

"Noooo." It was the last thing she heard from him as she swam away. Her laughter trailed behind her in the waves.

Continue the Ember Town series!

Book Six

Janavi

Order now at mj-james.com

Get a FREE Short Story!

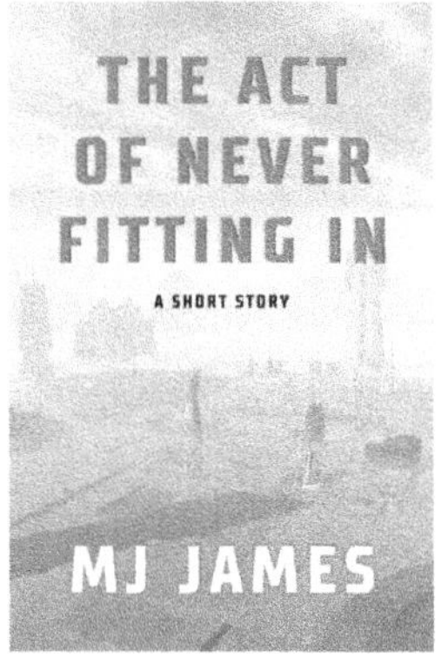

Join My Newsletter
Sign up at mj-james.com

ACKNOWLEDGMENTS

So much has changed since my last release, in the world and in my personal life. I am abstaining from marking any of the events as good or bad. They are a journey that I am taking. I am so honored that you are taking this journey with me.

Ember Town is my escape. It is my break from my science fiction that tends to be a bit darker, but it doesn't make it any less real or potent.

I want to thank everyone who has been on this journey with me from the start, as well as the new community I have found along the way.

To my kids, thank you for listening to me talk about my stories with an interest that only an autistic author can have. I am thankful for my beta readers: Mia, Lillian, and Maddie. Sam, thank you for your work with this series as my editor, Erica for stepping in to help catch any last errors, and Skye for giving a voice to my characters from the beginning.

A huge thank you to my readers. I wouldn't be able to keep writing without you. I appreciate all the support.

There is a reason that they keep trying to ban books - and that is because they have power. There is power in representation and seeing yourself on the page. There is also power in understanding perspectives other than your own. I will keep writing because I know it is one way of shining a light in all the darkness.

9 781958 175323